THE
DARK
WHISPER

ALSO BY BETHANY HELWIG

International Monster Slayers:
The Curse of Moose Lake
The Bite of Winter
The Ghosts of Yesteryear

~

Darkest Light

INTERNATIONAL MONSTER SLAYERS
~A GENNA BARNES NOVELLA~

THE DARK WHISPER

BETHANY HELWIG

BRIGHTWAY BOOKS

Copyright © 2018 by Bethany Helwig
Published by Brightway Books, LLC

Cover Illustration: Bethany Helwig

First Edition: May 2018

ISBN-10: 1-946639-12-5
ISBN-13: 978-1-946639-12-7

For those that always keep fighting
and never give up.

October 26, 1996

I stare at my bike in its bed of hay, a chain wrapped through its frame and locked to the wooden railing. I sit cross-legged on the dirt sprinkled floor and sigh, my chin resting heavy in my hands. It's hard to imagine the wind in my face, that feeling of being absolutely free, when I'm sitting on the cold floor of the barn with my source of freedom lying useless in front of me.

Two days. It's been *two whole days* since the last time I was allowed to ride it. It's been a longer punishment than the time I ran over Sprinkle's tail, the neighbor's stupid cat. Dad actually laughed when it happened. This time I don't even know what I did wrong. One second I'm racing my bike down the driveway chasing an imaginary monster with my wooden sword tucked into my belt; the next, Dad is running after me and pulls me to a stop.

"I'm sorry, Squirt," he said to me. "But you shouldn't be going out on rides right now."

I asked him why. He gave me a smile, patted me on the head, and just said I needed to stay close to the house. My bike, my unicorn I ride into battle against the foes of the driveway and the towering pines, has been chained to this railing ever since.

I grab the front wheel and spin it with a sigh, thinking of all my grand adventures I've had on it. Dad taught me how to ride. The other kids at school needed training wheels. I didn't. I had my Dad there the whole time until I could ride it all by myself. When I finally rode down the driveway, he ran beside me smiling the whole way. When we got back, he called me the conquering hero and Mom made lemon cake.

I nearly catch my fingers in the tire as I give it a good spin. I pat the seat gently, comforting my poor, trapped steed and start to sing it a lullaby to make it feel better. It must feel horrible being chained up, unable to break free.

"Genna!"

My mother's voice calls from outside the open door of the barn. Giving my bike one last pat with the promise of a quick return, I walk out of the barn dragging my feet, glide my hand along the side of Dad's car, and find Mom waiting for me. Her long black hair lifts in the wind like the wings of a crow about to fly away.

"I'm here," I mumble.

She kneels on the gravel driveway so she's at my height and brushes a warm hand over my cheek. "I told you to stay where I can see you while I'm tending the garden," she says. "What were you doing in the barn?"

"My unicorn's lonely," I say and point behind me where I can imagine a sad neigh from my trusty steed.

Mom smiles and rubs a finger above my eye. "Well, you've got grease on you. I think we better clean it off with a little dirt." She sticks her finger in the dirt and brushes it down my nose. It tickles and when she acts shocked at the dirt on my face, I giggle. "My little squirt in the dirt!"

"Mom!"

"Come here, you little squirt!"

She yanks me into her arms and finds all the spots I'm ticklish. I can't stop giggling and wiggle in her hold trying to escape. I try to tickle her back but she's not very ticklish. By the time she finally stops, I have to catch my breath. We both have dirt on us now, sitting in the driveway with our arms wrapped around each other.

Mom plants a kiss on top of my head. "I'm sorry your unicorn's lonely," she says. "Maybe I'll have to sing it a song so it doesn't feel so sad."

I lean back and frown. She's so silly. "It's not a *real* unicorn."

"Are you sure? I think it's starting to eat the hay."

"When can I ride my bike again?"

Her smile fades away. "Later, okay? It's not safe to be out right now."

"Why not?"

She pulls me close again and we rock back and forth slightly. Her body is warm against the cold breeze trying to pull away our matching black hair. I curl into her.

"You know what your daddy does, Genna. He protects people from monsters. Sometimes, we have to protect ourselves, too. And that means not going off by yourself, okay?"

I know the stories. I know the monsters that hide under beds are real. They aren't just stories that parents tell the other kids in my school. Werewolves live in our woods. They aren't all bad, but they aren't all good either. They aren't like the dogs my neighbor owns. There are bad things in this world. And my dad hunts them.

"Do you want to help me pick the rest of the tomatoes?" Mom asks.

I nod, ready to stay as close to my mother as possible now that I'm imagining wolf-men running through the woods that surround our home. She helps me up and takes me by the hand.

We're half way to the garden alongside the house when I hear a car coming up the driveway. We stop hand in hand as a van pulls to a stop in front of the house.

"Oh, no," I grumble.

My mom tugs at my hand. "They're not so bad."

"They broke my sword."

"That was an accident and your father made you a new one."

I pull my hand out of hers and cross my arms over my chest. I still liked my first sword better.

The doors of the van open and a man and woman step out—Mr. and Mrs. Mason. Mr. Mason's red hair makes his head look like it's on fire when the sun touches it. He's thin and gangly but there's always a smile on his face. Both he and his wife, a nice woman with bushy brown hair, wave at us as soon as they get out of the van. My mother winks at me and motions with one finger for me to follow her. Pouting, I stomp after her towards the van.

I hear the squeals and giggles before I see them. The

Masons open the next set of doors and out jump their two kids, a pair of red-haired pixies as my dad calls them. The next second they take off running towards the open door of the barn.

"Get back here!" Mr. Mason yells and sprints after them, all three disappearing into the barn.

"Don't touch my bike!" I shout with my hands cupped around my mouth, hoping they hear me. I'm about to march after them when I find my mother's hand on my shoulder holding me back. I glare up at her.

"Thanks for helping on such short notice." Mrs. Mason comes over and gives my mother a one-armed hug. "I know they're a handful."

"It's fine. I think Genna could use some friends around here right now."

"They're not my friends," I say loudly so it's very clear what I think about the twins. No one listens to me though. The Mason kids keep coming over no matter what I tell my mother.

"Be nice," my mother warns and gives my shoulder a gentle squeeze. "You get along just fine. You're just mad about the sword."

"No, I don't like them."

"*Genna.*"

Mrs. Mason laughs but the sound is short and she frowns when she thinks I'm not looking.

They start to talk quietly to each other but I can still hear.

"Jefferson found a possible lead," Mrs. Mason says to my mother, leaning in until their faces are close together. "The Grahams' son thinks he might have seen something before his sister was bitten. We're going to meet up with him at their house and—"

"Rosalyn?" I ask, even though I know they don't want me to hear. "Rosalyn was bitten?"

Mrs. Mason's eyes quickly turn to me and her face softens. "She was."

"So she's a werewolf?"

"Yes."

"But she's okay?"

"Yes."

Wow. Rosalyn, a werewolf. She's in my class at school but we aren't really friends. I wonder what that must be like to be able to turn into a wolf. It actually sounds pretty cool. My dad has warned me about werewolves but if they get medicine then they're okay. I hope Rosalyn got medicine. But what if she didn't? What if she went bad?

"Will she still go to school?" I ask with a frown.

They both smile down at me and my mother runs a hand through my hair.

"Later, once she's feeling better," she says.

Giggles interrupt the image in my head of becoming friends with Rosalyn so she can pull a sled while I ride it during winter. Mr. Mason comes out of the barn with a twin under each arm and they bat at each other across his belly.

"Stop it!" he says but can hardly be heard over the shrieks of his kids.

"If you don't knock it off right now," Mrs. Mason shouts in a tone my dad uses on me when I've broken the rules, "neither of you will be watching *Scooby-Doo* tonight!"

The shrieks instantly silence and Mr. Mason rolls his eyes before setting them on the ground before us. They both have pieces of straw sticking out of their hair and Phoenix has a smudge of dirt on her forehead. Next to their father, they're like a matching set of dolls with their red hair and freckles.

Mr. Mason moves past me to put his arm around his wife's waist. "We need to get going."

"Right." Mrs. Mason ruffles the twins' hair and stares them down. "You both be good for Andromeda, okay? She'll tell me if you've been trying to trap squirrels again or using permanent marker on Genna. Then it's no *Scooby-Doo* for life."

Their green eyes go wide in fear and they nod.

"We'll be back tonight," Mr. Mason says. Then they hurry to their van and leave the four of us behind.

Mom slings her arms around the three of us, pushing me up against Hawk. He pulls his shoulders in like I have cooties. But that's just dumb. Cooties aren't real.

"Okay, who wants popcorn?" Mom asks.

The twins leap out of her arms, strike a pose with their hands raised to the sky and scream in unison "POPCORN!" before making a mad dash for the house. My mother nudges me with a wink and I race after, quickly outstripping the twins but then we stop to fight at the door handle and burst into the kitchen in a tangle.

Several really, really long minutes later, we share a big bowl of popcorn outside next to the garden as Mom pulls weeds and lays down a blanket to "let the flowers sleep through winter." What we really want, though, is the show. Whenever there is popcorn, there is a show. Sure enough, when the weeds are pulled and most of the garden is covered, my mother motions us over.

"Here we go," Hawk whispers to his sister and they cram popcorn into their mouths.

Mom waves her hand over the soil like a magician from that cartoon I watched a few nights ago. The dirt shakes and a sprout of green coils up out of the ground. It twists and climbs higher as Mom spins her hands around it. It gets bigger and bigger until a great purple flower bursts from the top.

"Woooooow!" the twins say and popcorn falls from their mouths in awe. A smile stays on my face as my mother makes the flower change color, then sprouts a few more and has them dance together. We clap our hands and squeal as the flowers reach out their leaves like hands to tickle us.

Mom is special. There's no one else like her. She can make plants grow, make them big, make them small, make them move, make them bloom. Our garden is always growing until winter comes. Even then, even when it's coldest and snow buries the world, a flower can grow.

When it starts to get dark, Mom says the show is over and Hawk throws a fit. Phoenix, even though she's disappointed too, tells him to knock it off. Eventually he calms down and we move inside to play heroes and monsters. We fight over who is supposed to be the hero because no one wants to be the monster until Mom leaps out of her bedroom wrapped in a blanket and shrieks at us.

"I am the traveling troll!" she cries and holds her hands like deadly claws. "Come to take your toys!"

I draw my wooden sword and hold it high to the ceiling. "Stop, troll! You can't take our toys!"

We fight the troll, then the vampire, and the evil wizard before riding the centaur round and round and round.

We're in the middle of flying on the back of a dragon when someone knocks on the door. Mom hushes us and has us move back as she goes to see who it is. Just before she opens the door, she puts her hand on the shotgun hidden above the door. She and Dad are the only ones allowed to touch it. Guns are not toys. I know what they are and what they do. I'm not allowed near them.

She opens the door and the Masons come in. Phoenix rushes over but Hawk throws his sword down and puts his hands on his hips.

"We were flying to the moon!" he yells.

Just then Dad walks in and tosses his baseball hat onto the kitchen table. "Some other time, kids, when you've got oxygen masks."

The twins eyeball my dad like he's crazy but I jump up and hurry to him. He bends down and scoops me up into a bear hug.

"And how's my squirt in the dirt?" he says and brushes something off my face with rough fingers. "Did you bury your head in the driveway? Look at you." He bounces me a few times in his arms and we watch the Masons try to wrangle the twins. "Were you the pilot to the moon?"

I nod and wrap my arms around my dad's neck, suddenly very tired.

"That's my girl," he says as he rests his cheek against the top of my head. "The birdies here would probably crash if they were in charge."

I smile and give a great, big yawn.

"I think it's time for bed," Mom says and comes over to rub my arm.

"I'm not tired," I say.

My protests don't stop my father from carrying me into my bedroom. He sets me down then leaves to help the Masons get their kids in their van while Mom helps me into my pajamas.

"I can do it myself," I grumble and force my arms through the sleeves of my Wonder Woman pajamas.

"I know you can," Mom says and boops my nose with her finger. "What book do you want tonight?"

"*The Hobbit*!"

She laughs and walks to the bookshelf at the foot of my bed. The front door slams and a few seconds later Dad walks in running a hand through his hair. Mom finds the well-used book and passes it to him. He looks at the cover and shakes his head.

"How on earth is a seven-year-old able to understand this kind of stuff yet?" he grumbles and motions for me to scoot over on my bed. I shuffle to the side, pulling my blankets with me, and he takes a seat on the edge of my mattress.

"I thought you liked dragons," he says. "You want to keep reading this one where they go on a journey to kill one?"

"Not all dragons are good. Just like people. Just like werewolves."

He blinks. "You're a crazy smart kid, you know that? You got your brain from your mother."

"And your stubbornness from your father," Mom says from the doorway. "Goodnight, Genna."

"Night, Mom."

Dad thumbs to the beginning and starts to read. His gruff voice lulls me to sleep almost instantly. When I wake up again, Dad's gone and my room is dark. I blink groggily with my stuffed platypus tucked in my arms and my blankets pulled up to my chin. The glow of my Scooby-Doo nightlight is overwhelmed by the bright light shining beneath my door. Still half-asleep, I slip out of my blankets and trudge flat-footed to the door. I crack it open a few inches so I can peer into the kitchen beyond.

"I don't know but I intend to find out," Dad whispers to my mother. "We almost had him, Andromeda. I know I tagged him in the shoulder when he bolted. If we can just find out who is suffering from a shoulder injury—"

"And you have to leave right now?" Mom asks.

"This is the closest we've ever been. Mary is going to meet me over there while Robin watches their kids." He slings on his jacket and tucks a gun into the holster at his side. "Make sure you have a hand on the guns."

"I know. Be safe, Jeff." She perches up on her toes and I look away just as they kiss. Ew. When I peer back through the door again, Dad is gone and Mom stands alone in the kitchen. I watch as she moves to the windows and tests the locks, then does the same to the door, and eventually walks over to my bedroom. I run back to my bed, fly under the covers, and pretend to be asleep when she walks in. After testing my window too, she tucks something underneath my bed, then sits next to me to lay a hand on my forehead.

"Mom's going to sleep in here tonight with you, okay?" she whispers.

Forgetting to pretend to be asleep, I nod. She curls up on my bed that's much too small for her and tucks in around me, her arms holding me close to her. Not sure what's going on, I drift asleep in my mother's arms.

The next time I wake up is to the front door creaking

open and my mother putting a hand over my mouth. She shushes me and tells me to keep still. I do as she says even though my heart starts to race in my chest. What's going on?

I hear footsteps in the kitchen but there's too many for it to just be Dad returning home. Maybe he came here with Mrs. Mason? But there's a strange clicking, like dragon talons on the kitchen tiles. Mom slips out of my bed and pulls out something from underneath the mattress. She holds her hand out to me and I quickly wrap mine around her own. She helps me off the bed and then puts her lips to my ear.

"Hide under the bed, Genna," she whispers. "Hurry. Don't make a sound."

I'm trembling as I get down on my hands and knees. She helps push aside a few forgotten toys so I can shimmy underneath. I press back until I meet the wall and tuck my arms in to my chest. Mom shuffles away from the bed, pulls my potted plant off my dresser, and scoots it towards the door of my room. Waving one hand over it like the magician, the tendrils grow amazingly fast and spread across the floor like octopus limbs.

I hold my breath as the door slowly creaks open and dark shapes loom in the entrance. My mother hides against the dresser and waits as three wolves sneak into my bedroom. As soon as their paws cross the plant limbs, the tendrils suddenly come alive and wrap themselves around the wolves.

The sound of it is horrible. The wolves spit and snarl and chomp their teeth at the vines quickly wrapping around them. I clamp my hands over my ears as another sound drowns out all the others. A gunshot. My mother has a gun in her hands and fires again and again until I can't hear a thing. Two of the wolves stop moving. The third keeps trying to chew free of the vines around its throat. I don't realize I'm screaming until my mother leans down sharply to make sure I'm okay.

The window breaks and glass scatters across the floor as another massive shape jumps through it and lands on top of my mother. The gun skids across the floor and ends up within arm's reach beneath my bed.

I know what I have to do. I need to be brave like my mother, like my father.

My fingers curl around the grip of the gun and I scoot forward so I can aim the deadly thing at the monsters attacking my mother. I squeeze on the trigger but I'm not strong enough. I grimace and tears run down my face as I fight and fight that trigger with my small fingers that can barely fit around it.

The gun jerks so hard when it fires that my hands hit the frame of the bed and I whack my head. Ears ringing and head spinning, I'm not sure what happens next. Pain throbs in my hands and I'm dragged forward by what feels like daggers digging into my arm. When I come to, I'm lying on my back in my bedroom next to my mother with her bloody arms wrapped around me. A shape looms in the doorway— black fur, yellow eyes of the devil, and blood-stained teeth— before it turns around and vanishes, taking the last surviving wolf with it.

"You're safe, baby girl," my mother wheezes. "I've got you."

"Mom. It hurts."

"I know, baby, I know." She tugs me closer to her chest. Her breaths are shallow and fast and she groans. "Genna, I need you to get the phone. Call your father. Can you do that for me?"

I nod and push myself shakily into a sitting position, my mother's hands guiding me. When I look back at her on the floor, I choke on a sob. There's blood everywhere, tufts of fur, and the roots my mother had used as weapons lie useless beside her.

"*Mom.*"

"Go, Genna."

I rise to my feet and clutch my hot burning arm to my stomach as I make for the kitchen. When I almost fall, I lean one shoulder against the counter and scoot along until I reach the phone. Wrapping my bloody fingers around it, I shake so much I can't dial the right number.

I'm in the middle of redialing when two figures slip in through the open front door with guns raised. I drop the phone and push up against the counter before I realize it's Dad and Mr. Mason.

"Genna!" Dad shouts and rushes for me. He kneels and pulls back my sleeve so he can see the ugly, bleeding bite mark beneath. "No, no, no . . ."

"Dad!" I point towards the bedroom. "Mom's hurt. You have to help her."

He grabs my shoulders. "Stay *right* here with Robin."

Then he leaps up and runs into the bedroom. Mr. Mason hurries forward to take my father's place. But I don't want to stay here. I want to help. I want to know my mother's going to be okay. I try to walk into the bedroom but Mr. Mason wraps his arms around me to hold me back.

"You shouldn't go in there," he says. "Now, I need to give you a shot, okay? I need to give you medicine for that bite."

"I want to see my Mom!"

I fight against him and start to scream as he wrestles with me. He manages to tuck me in tight to his chest and keeps an arm around me so no matter how much I thrash, I can't get free.

"It's going to be okay. It's going to be okay." He says it over and over and over again as he pulls a black pen out of his pocket and hits it hard to my leg. I screech as the needle pricks my skin. My spine tingles while the rest of me burns. There's too much pain and I'm too hot. Still keeping a hold on me, Mr. Mason bends lower, opens the cabinet under the sink, and pulls out a plastic box. He continues to murmur to me that everything is going to be okay as he pulls out a long white bandage and wraps it around my arm.

Mr. Mason rises but keeps me locked against him as we walk together into the bedroom. My bare feet get sticky with blood on the floor. Dad has Mom in his arms sitting partway up. Her whole body shakes and she clutches onto my father as if she's going to be ripped away from him.

Dad looks up, tears running down his face. "Is she okay?"

"I gave her the serum and wrapped her arm," Mr. Mason says. "We have maybe ten minutes."

"She shouldn't be here for this."

I finally slip out of Mr. Mason's hold and lurch forward to my mother. I kneel beside her and take her trembling hand in mine.

She tries to smile at me. "My little squirt in the dirt. I love you so much."

My father strokes her hair and says softly, "Andromeda."

I've never been so afraid in my entire life.

I know what this is. I've seen the movies, I've read the books, I've caught glimpses of it on the news.

My mother is dying.

"There has to be something we can do," Dad whispers and his voice cracks. He's not supposed to break. My father is made of steel and iron. Nothing can stop him. He's a hero.

"I can feel it," Mom says and sounds sick. "I'm not going to turn. I'm not going to make it."

I grip her hand more tightly. "Don't say that, Mom."

"I love you. I love you both," she says. She keeps my hand in hers but leans her face into Dad's chest.

Dad repeats the words back to her over and over again as he clutches her closer to him, tears sliding down his face.

Everything's wrong. This can't happen. It can't. And this pain inside—it *hurts*. It hurts so badly that I squeeze my mother's hand as I curl up on myself.

"She needs to go," Mr. Mason says behind us. "Genna—"

"No!" I shout and tuck in closer to my mother. "I won't leave her!"

Mom turns her head in my direction with tears and a smile. Even like this she's beautiful. She's always been so beautiful and strong. I want to be just like her when I grow up—I want *her* there when I grow up.

"Listen to me," Mom says with a grimace. "No matter where you are, no matter what you become, I will always love you. Remember that whenever you're lost or afraid or feel alone. You will always have me here."

She pushes her finger gently to my heart then swipes that same finger down my nose like she always does when she puts dirt on me. I sob and try to hold her hand again when the pain in my chest makes me double over and I let out a pained growl.

"She has to go," Mr. Mason says more urgently.

Dad looks at me and says weakly, "Go."

"No!"

Mr. Mason wraps his arms around my middle and hauls me up.

"NO!"

I flail and kick as my entire body shakes, my fingers and toes burning like I've stuck them in a fire. Mr. Mason backs out of the room.

"NOOOO!"

My legs crack and I let out an ear-splitting scream at the pain of it. My arms and legs convulse on their own, my back cracks a hundred times, and every part of me feels wrong. The lights are too bright, every sound too loud, every sensation too much. Mr. Mason hauls me into Mom and Dad's bedroom.

As my screams change into howls and every part of me becomes a monster, he slams the door shut and locks us inside.

October 31, 1996
Day 0

It should be raining. It shouldn't be sunny and nice out as if the world is perfectly okay. I press my forehead against the cold glass as I watch the sunlight move slowly through the lifeless trees. Most of the leaves have fallen and only a few hold on desperately to their branches as if unwilling to let go. I know how they feel.

It's been a week since . . . since everything changed. I can't get myself to do much except stare out the window. Dad's been trying so hard to be there for me, I know he has. He's stayed with me during every transformation, stroked my black fur, whispered that it's going to be okay somehow. He's going to put a stop to that werewolf that took everything from us.

But there's something in his face when he looks at me when I have four paws, a muzzle, tail, and fur. There are tears that don't fall but remain there, watery and held captive in his eyes. After that first night, I haven't cried once. I feel shriveled up inside.

I'll never hear my mother sing again or have her braid my hair.

She's gone.

Yesterday I watched as her coffin was lowered into the ground. The funeral wasn't long and the crowd was small. The Masons were there. The twins for once weren't bouncing around as if they ate a bunch of sugar. They must have known what was going on. Dad held my hand, Hawk took the other, and Phoenix his so we stood in a chain of linked hands.

But I still felt so alone.

"Genna?"

I don't move at the sound of my name. Why bother?

"You should eat something, baby girl."

A hand rests on my shoulder and I look out of the corner of my eye to find Dad standing next to me. He looks tired.

I shake my head and stare out the window again. "No thanks."

He sits beside me in the bay window. We've been staying at the Wicks for the last week. I couldn't sleep in the cabin. I can't be anywhere near that place anymore. The Masons offered to make room for us but with the energetic twins, I certainly didn't want to. I guess Dad didn't either so here we are. There's a smell of cows here I can't escape. I had never noticed it before but I've been smelling a lot of weird things lately that I never used to be able to—like Dad. He smells like pine needles, coffee, and aftershave. My new wolf nose is sensitive.

"Genna," he says and rubs my shoulder in small circles. "I . . . I'm here for you. You know that, right?"

"Why did Mom die?" I ask suddenly. The thought has been on my mind since that night. "The werewolf bit both of us. I didn't die. Why did Mom?"

He takes a long time to answer and continues those small circles on my shoulder. "Your mother was special. Very special. Blessed. And what made her special—"

"Magic."

"Yes, magic. It—well, it doesn't get along with what makes a werewolf a werewolf. Her body couldn't handle it and—" He stops and takes a long shaky breath.

A horrible thought occurs to me. "Would Mom not get along with me then?"

He suddenly clutches me tight to his chest and rocks me gently. "Oh, baby girl, no. That's not what I meant. There's nothing in this world that would ever make her stop loving you."

I think about that night again and shudder. "I miss her."

Dad kisses the top of my head. "So do I."

We stay that way for a long time, arms wrapped around each other and staring out the window at the sad trees and fallen leaves. It feels like hours until Dad finally gets up and tells me he needs to get to work but the Wicks will take care of me. I spend the rest of the day at that window. Mrs. Wick comes by around supper time and asks if I want to eat with them at the table. I don't answer. A while later Mr. Wick asks if I'd like to help take care of the cows with him. I say no and they leave me be.

Dad comes back during the evening as it finally starts to rain big, fat drops outside. He shakes out his jacket and comes to sit with me again at the window. We don't say much of anything but watch the rain as the light quickly fades.

The phone rings. Two seconds later, Mrs. Wick shouts, "Jefferson! *Jefferson!*"

She sounds terrified and appears around the corner holding out the receiver for the phone with the cord stretched as far as it can go. Dad launches to his feet and immediately takes the phone from her.

"Hello? Mary?" His eyes go wide. "Come again? I'll be right—Mary? *Mary!*" He passes the phone back to Mrs. Wick and whispers something urgently to her before he races to my side.

"Genna, I have to go help the Masons."

"Are they okay?"

"I don't know." He kneels so he's looking up at me and grasps both of my arms. "I need you to stay here with Mrs. Wick, okay? She'll take care of you. I'll be right back."

"Dad, what's going on?"

"Just stay here. I love you." He kisses my forehead and sprints for the door, yanking his jacket off the hook on the wall, and vanishing outside. I realize my hands are shaking. Horrible images come to mind of what could be happening. Are the Masons being attacked like Mom and I were? Have wolves come into their home? I squeeze my eyes shut as I think of monsters biting those little twins and attacking Mr. and Mrs. Mason.

I find Mrs. Wick beside me in an instant.

"I'm sure everything's going to be fine," she says and guides me over to the big recliner in front of the tube television. "Take a seat. There you go. Would you like some hot chocolate? I'll go make some. That'll make you feel better."

She grabs a quilt from the couch and drapes it over my shoulders before she hustles to the kitchen. I try to sit patiently as I knead my knuckles into my thighs and keep an eye on the dark window as it's lashed with rain. Is Dad going to be okay? Are the Masons? Am I?

Glasses and dishes clink in the kitchen but apart from that and the rain, it's too quiet. A shiver runs down my spine and the hair sticks up on the back of my neck. I'm too still. I need to move. I throw off the blanket and start to pace in front of the television. A floorboard creaks to the rhythm of me going back and forth and back and forth. Suddenly I find that pacing is not enough. No, I need to *move*. I need to leave. I don't know why. I don't like the thought of going out into the rain but I have to. I just do.

As I walk to the door, I feel the change come over me. Pain grips me as my limbs distort, my senses warp, and I buckle down onto all fours. Fur sprouts all over my body and my clothes vanish as if sunken beneath my heavy black coat. I hiss and snarl at the pain of the transformation. It must alert Mrs. Wick because she flies out the kitchen with a gasp.

"Genna!" she shouts.

Before she can say anything more, I ram my shoulder into the door—possessing strength I didn't even know I have—and race out into the rain.

I run. My mind empties and there's nothing except the movement of limbs, the plink of rain, the splash of water as my paws go through puddles, my panting breaths. My sharp eyes find paths through the darkness and storm and my footfalls are sure. Every now and then my ears twitch as I catch the sounds of other animals nearby.

With the long strides of a wolf, I charge ahead. I don't know where I'm going, just that I need to get there as soon as possible. There's a terrible danger nearby and I need to move as fast as my canine legs can carry me. There's no thought of Dad far behind me, the Masons, of home.

The world passes with a blur and even my own mind seems to shrink away. Genna the little girl is replaced by Genna the beast.

Then as if a switch is flipped, I return to myself. I come to an abrupt halt as my legs shake. The pain comes again as my black fur disappears, my limbs break and change, and I stand in the middle of a dark and unknown wood alone.

I don't know where I am. Wherever "here" is, it's dark, cold, and smells like dirt. Moonlight turns the tall daunting silhouettes of the trees into waving, creaking fingers of the boogeyman come to gobble me up. Out of breath and dizzy, I take a seat on the damp soil of the forest. It's no longer raining or I've run so far that I've outpaced the rain. Even so, I'm cold. So cold now. I shiver and wrap my arms around my legs, tucking my knees in to my chest to stave off the chill. I find that my hands are covered in drying mud and my shoes look just as dirty.

Why did I run? I don't understand what happened. Dad must be so worried. I have to get back somehow—but I don't know how. Which way do I go now? Or should I stay here and wait? Is Moose Lake close by? But it feels like I've been running for days. Where am I?

I put my chin on my knees and start to rock back and forth as I hum a song Mom sings—*used* to sing. She's gone and I'm lost. The force of it hits me like a boulder to my chest and tears roll down my cheeks as I continue to hum. As I think about Mom, of all the things I miss so much already, I stop humming. When I close my eyes I can see her dying in Dad's arms.

A branch snaps nearby. I freeze to listen. There's a—a *smell.* I sniff a few times and wipe the tears from my face. Then I hear it. Footsteps. They shuffle far too close for comfort. Strange noises and smells in the dead of night in an unknown place are not something I want. I uncoil my arms from around my legs and plant my hands on the ground so I can leap away in a hurry if I need to. I hold my breath and listen to those footsteps come closer.

But what if it's Dad? He could have followed me somehow.

"Hello?" I call. "Is someone there?"

"Who's there?"

Not Dad. A boy. Disappointment settles in my chest.

Through the darkness a pale yellow light appears. It comes closer a little at a time. It's shaped weird like a small airplane.

"Where are you?" the boy calls.

He sounds like a kid. Not a monster or a dangerous creature.

"Over here," I say louder.

The glowing airplane comes closer until I realize it's a glow-in-the-dark shirt the boy is wearing. I wave to get his attention and through the darkness he must finally see me. He comes within a few feet and then stops. I can hardly see what he looks like but he's short, maybe my height. The outline of his hair is shaggy. His white shoes gleam in the moonlight.

"Where are we?" he asks.

"I don't know. How did *you* get here?"

"I ran."

"Me too."

Does that mean . . . is he a werewolf too? He comes closer and takes a seat beside me. I wrinkle my nose. That smell I picked up was definitely him—foul and dirty.

"Really?" he asks.

"Yeah." I fold my hands together in my lap and act the way my mother would want me too—politely. "What's your name?"

"James."

"I'm Genna. So we're both lost?"

"I guess." He sniffles loudly. "Can I . . . can I hold your hand?"

He sounds so scared. I guess I am too, so I reach across the space between us and our hands fumble about until we find each other.

"Are you okay?" I ask. "Are you hurt?"

"I'm scared."

"Me too." I scoot across the dirt towards him until my knee touches his. "At least we're not alone anymore." Saying the words out loud makes me feel a little better.

"I want to go home," James says and his voice quavers.

Rallying what courage I have, I say, "Then we'll go home. My dad will find us."

"But—" When he starts to sob, I squeeze his hand to comfort him. Eventually he takes a deep breath and says, "I don't know where my house is."

"It's okay." Feeling rather clever and proud, I lift up my shoe to pull back the tongue. I try to show him what's written on it. "I have my address written in my shoe. If we can get there then we can find someone who knows where you live. We're going to get home, James. You and me."

"How?"

"My dad will save us." Trying to sound brave, I add, "Or we'll just have to get there ourselves. We can do it. Once it's light again, we'll find out where we are." I hold my free hand up to him. "Pinky swear, okay? I pinky swear I'm going to get us both home."

He holds out his pinky and I give it a good shake with my own.

"See?" I say. "We're going to be okay."

We both fall silent and sit together holding hands as we wait for the sun to rise. I'll wait for it all night if I have to, but waiting takes a long time and the sun doesn't want to come up. I wait and wait and James ends up curled up next to me with his head on my shoulder. I stay awake to keep him safe. That's what Dad does for others. That's what I'm going to do for him.

Creatures move nearby in the darkness, crumpling leaves and rustling grass, so I keep very still and quiet. When a squirrel starts chirping at us, I nearly jump but James sleeps on.

My eyelids grow heavy as the night wears on and my head nods. I almost fall asleep with my head resting on top of the boy's when I see a light in the distance. A flashlight. I prod James awake with my elbow and we watch the light come closer. James lurches to his feet as he suddenly wakes but I grab the back of his pants and pull him back down. We ought to be careful.

"We don't know who that is," I hiss at him.

Then I hear it—a man calling our names along with a bunch of other kids echoing his words. If there's a bunch of kids with him, he must be okay, right?

"Come on." I haul James to his feet.

"Over here!" he yells.

The flashlight turns in our direction. We wave our hands to be seen and walk towards our rescuer through tall grass and bushes.

"Kids!" the man calls. "I'm so glad I found you!"

Struggling through a tangle of nettles, we at last reach the man and find seven other kids with him—all dirty, scared, and huddled together. Did they run off and get lost like James and me? Are they werewolves?

The man kneels so he's at our level and tilts the flashlight to illuminate his face. There's something familiar about him. I feel like I know those bright blue eyes, the wild dark hair, the dimpled smile.

"Hey, it's okay," he says and gives each of us a pat on the shoulder. "I'm going to take care of you. I know you're scared but everything's going to be all right. I've got you."

He keeps on smiling and the other kids bunch up around him, watching me and James.

"How do you know our names?" I ask. "Did my dad send you?"

His smile fades and he takes my hand. "I know your name, Genevieve, because I'm like you. I know what you are. And I'm going to take care of you."

"We want to go home," I say and point between James and me.

"I know, sweetheart, but it's dangerous right now."

"Why?"

"Because *you* are dangerous. Think about it, Genevieve. You couldn't stop yourself from running all the way out here. You couldn't control changing into a wolf. If you go back home, what if you can't stop yourself from attacking your father? Do you want that?"

My throat feels tight and my lower lip starts to tremble as I recall the wolves bursting into our house and attacking my mother. I don't ever want to be the one to do that to someone else.

"No," I say weakly.

"Then let me help you," he says. "I can teach you to control all of it."

I'm not supposed to trust strangers but part of me knows that I should. That surety grows stronger and stronger until there is no fear, no worry, no doubt. I will trust this man. I must.

"Okay," I say and take James's hand in mine again. "What's your name?"

The man's smile returns. "You can call me Dasc."

James gives me an encouraging nod as if to let me know we ought to trust this man. But I already feel it. I *know* it. This man can be trusted.

"How did you find us?" I ask.

He tilts his head to the side like Mr. Wick's dog when it hears a strange sound.

"I was in the area visiting an old friend when I heard you kids crashing through the woods. I followed your scent until I found you."

"No."

"No what?"

I frown. "You were calling for us. That's how you found us. Why were you calling for us if you could just smell us?"

His eyes go up and down me as if finding something odd. "You're a clever girl. I was calling your names so I wouldn't frighten you." He suddenly straightens and holds out his hand. "Come on. It's not safe here."

"Why not?"

"Because there are things out here that hunt werewolves." He glances towards the sky and I can't help but look too as if I'll find some beast flying down to carry us away. "Don't worry. You're safe as long as you're with me. You believe me, don't you?"

"Yes," James says without hesitation.

I don't know why or how, but I do. I do trust this stranger. "Yes," I say subdued.

He rises to his feet. "Then come on. We have a long ways to go yet and not a lot of time."

"Where are we going?" I ask as he takes my hand.

"Somewhere safe. A place for people like us."

"A place for monsters?" I whisper.

He nods and gives me a warm smile. "A place for monsters."

November 5, 1996
Day 5

I quickly learn to dread the Fridge. It's not an actual fridge but that's what everyone in the compound calls it. It sits in the heart of the web of tunnels beneath the frozen forest above—my temporary home. The reality is the Fridge is a metal cage they put the kids—like me—into when we transform. We aren't ready to control ourselves yet and it's for everyone's protection as well as our own. It's our place of timeout.

But I can't understand it. The whole time I ran up here after I met Dasc I felt like I could control myself as a wolf. I felt a little beastly but I thought I was okay. But now that I'm here, I can't seem to control myself at all.

The first time I shifted after I got to this underground camp in the middle of nowhere, I got angry real fast, I couldn't think straight, and tried to make a break for it.

That's when the adults shifted and managed to drag me into the Fridge. The cage only seemed to make things worse. I knew what it was to be a trapped animal. I gnawed on the metal bars until my gums began to bleed. I tried to dig a hole only to find more bars underneath. I howled, I barked, I snarled, but still they kept me locked up. All the while on the other side of the bars, a pack of the adult wolves laid around the cage in a circle as if to keep me company or make sure I didn't escape. It wasn't until I fell asleep then woke again as a little girl that they let me out.

Dasc showed up soon after as I was given a bowl of soup and sat with me on a log in the main hub of the tunnels. He said encouraging things, that the Fridge was necessary, that I wouldn't need to go back in once I could control myself, that he hated having to put anyone in there, but everyone's safety was his concern.

I've been put in the Fridge three more times since then.

This is the fourth.

I wake from my fitful sleep and find furless hands at the end of my arms. On the other side of the bars there's a timber wolf watching me intently with grey eyes. She's been my ever watchful guardian, assigned to me since I got here.

"Can you let me out, please?" I croak, finding my throat rather dry.

She puts her nose against the lock on the gate and lifts it open. I'm quick to scamper out and escape the nightmare cage. In need of something to hug, I launch myself forward onto my guardian and wrap my arms around her thick furry neck.

"I'm hungry," I whisper.

She huffs in the way that wolves do and nudges me with

her nose. At her urging, I get up, one hand still clenched in her fur, and follow her out of the room—not that I can go without her. Everywhere I go an adult is always present, each and every one of them a werewolf like me. Except unlike me, none of them want to leave this place.

An ache grows powerfully painful in my chest. I miss Dad. I miss Mom. I miss home. I don't know how long I'm going to have to stay here until they think I can control myself. They keep telling me it will take time, but how much time? No one answers that question.

We walk through the tunnel with low ceilings and enter the "Den" as they like to call it. It's the largest of the caves where everyone gathers. The walls are mostly smooth but there are little tendrils of plant roots sticking through the ceiling and every now and then if someone barks too loud, bits of dirt might sprinkle you on the head. Hay and dry grass cover the edges of the room but the middle is packed down around a stone ring that holds the cooking fire. It's warmer in here and tendrils of smoke drift up to vanish through vents to the outside.

"Genna!"

I turn at the sound of my name and find James waving me over to sit with him and a group of other kids. Their guardians lay and sit in a loose ring nearby as always. I join James while my guardian wolf joins the adults. I sit down and take a bowl of stew from another boy with a quiet thank you.

"You just got out?" James asks in an undertone.

I nod. "You?"

"A few minutes ago."

"I hate going into the Fridge."

"Me too." He slurps at his own stew then whispers. "Have you gotten any better? You know, at controlling it?"

I shake my head and glower at the food cupped in my hands. "I don't know how. I wish they'd tell us how they do it so we could leave."

Next to me a small boy with watery eyes and a runny nose whispers, "I don't want to be here. I want to go home." He stretches out a shaky hand and wraps it around mine. He's the smallest of us, and the one usually bursting into tears randomly. Kelsey.

Rosalyn, a girl with long brown hair on my other side leans over to say, "I think we're safer here."

"You don't want to go home?" I ask.

Her hands tremble and her stew slops off her spoon as she tries to take a mouthful. "I don't want to be a monster. People hunt monsters. But these people seem nice enough."

"What about your parents?"

"What about yours? Didn't you say your dad is some kind of monster killer?"

I glower at her. "My dad doesn't kill werewolves, Rosalyn."

She shrugs and keeps eating.

Despite her talk, I know that she misses her home too. I've heard her crying in the night and caught her staring off towards the exit. She talks like she's tough but she's really not.

While we eat, a group gathers near the entrance and we stop to watch what's going on. A couple of men and women haul in cardboard boxes and set them in a pile in the middle of the room next to the open fire pit. One man stands taller than the rest and his eyes scan each person in the room, eventually staring at us kids. He walks over and our guardians immediately stand like soldiers when their commanding officer appears.

"Whisper," our guardians murmur and nod to him as this man stops to inspect us.

"Hello, everyone. My name is Alex," he says. His voice is quiet as if he's afraid to talk too loud but there's something about his tone that makes me feel very small. "While Dasc is away, I'm in charge of everyone here."

"Where is he?" I blurt out.

His eyes lock onto me and my face grows warm.

"He's out keeping us safe. There have been a few wendigos roaming too close nearby and he's gone to take care of them."

Rosalyn raises a shaky hand as if she's in class. "What's a—a win—"

"It's a monster," he says flatly. "Something that looks like it could've been human once but has eaten so many lost hikers and gnawed on their bones that its teeth are jagged and it's gone freakishly pale. They're clever devils with long, thin hands that can choke the life out of a cougar."

The blood drains from my face. James wraps his hand around mine while Kelsey squeezes the life out of my other one.

"It's a dangerous world," Alex continues. "But we're here to protect you. Dasc is here to protect you." He scans us one more time. "Come on. I just brought in a batch of supplies. You all look like you could use a good bath and fresh clothes. We'll take care of your dirty things."

My heart thunders in my chest and my palms go sweaty. I don't want them to take any of my things. My mom and dad gave me my glittery shirt, Woman Wonder shoes, patched jeans, and wool jacket. The clothes remind me that I don't belong here. This place isn't home. It's unfamiliar and scary and I just want what I know. I clutch onto my jacket with both hands as my guardian comes over to usher me to the sleeping areas.

The rest of the kids and I are escorted along while some of the adults carry boxes in after us. We split into the girl and boy caves before our guardians start offering us clothes.

My guardian tries to push a shirt into my arms. "Your stuff is filthy, honey."

I shake my head vigorously and she sighs.

"You don't need to be afraid. Look, this shirt has a nice rainbow pattern on it. Do you like rainbows?"

I shake my head again. I like unicorns, and Dad says that unicorns really don't like rainbows because elves tease them about it. I wonder if my unicorn bike is still chained up in the barn at home . . .

"What about this one?" she asks and holds up a purple long-sleeve shirt with a horse on the front.

I run a hand down it. It feels soft and smells clean. When I take a deep breath, I realize just how much I stink. My guardian smiles and puts her hands on my shoulders.

"Why don't you pick out what you like and you can change over there?" She points to a corner of the room shielded by a curtain hanging from the ceiling. "There's some water so you can wash up. I'll wash your old things and give them back to you, okay?"

I guess that doesn't sound too bad since she's going to

be bringing them back. Slowly releasing the tight grip on my jacket, I dig through the box of girl's clothes. I take the horse shirt, jeans, socks, underwear, and a fluffy gray jacket.

She pushes a pair of dark tennis shoes into my arms as well. "Take these too. Your shoes are going to get holes in them soon."

Before I can argue, she picks up the box and points to the corner. Holding the new bundle of clothes and shoes tight to my chest, I turn around and shuffle behind the curtain. Rosalyn and a couple other girls are already back here peeling off their smelly socks and shirts and getting into metal tubs of water. I hide behind the last tub and pull off my worn shoes. After making sure no one is looking, I tug at the tongue of my shoe with my address written on it in my dad's handwriting. It takes a bit of work but I eventually manage to yank it off. I'm pretty sure I can remember my address, but what if I forget? I promised James I would get us both home. I need to know where home is.

Putting my old shoes aside, I tuck the little cloth tag into my new pair of socks and get out of the rest of my dirty clothes. The water in the tub is actually pretty warm and I sink into it until my chin hovers at the surface. For a while I just sit there and watch as clouds of dirt rise off my skin and spread slowly through the water. I *am* dirty.

My guardian suddenly appears through the part in the curtain and scoops up my old things. I startle and splash some water onto the floor.

"It's okay," she says. "I'm just going to get them washed." She disappears again.

I start to breathe fast as I panic so I close my eyes and think of when my mother would give me baths. We would race plastic dolphins back and forth to the ends of the tub. I would pretend they were selkies and swap them out for dolls to come on dry land on the edge of the tub. She'd sing me a song she said that the selkies made and would trail bubbles down my nose with her finger.

In this strange place far away from everything I know, I hum that song and absentmindedly stroke a finger down my nose.

The water grows cold before I finally scrub at myself and dunk my hair. My guardian comes back with a towel before leaving me to dry off and put on my new clothes. I double check to make sure the tag with the address for home is secure in my sock before slipping it on and tying the laces of my tennis shoes.

I'm guided out to what the adults call the "play room." The cave walls are painted bright colors, there are cushy mats on the floor, and hundreds of worn toys litter the room—little train engines, patched teddy bears, and building blocks with claw marks on them. The rest of the kids are already here. Our guardians pull out toys and try to get us to play with them or each other. I take a seat next to James and we silently observe everyone else, not caring to try to take part. Rosalyn wears a sad face as she sorts the building blocks into a tower which she then knocks over before building it up once more. She repeats this over and over again. Kelsey sits in a corner clutching a teddy bear to his chest as his guardian talks quietly to him.

I don't understand why they want us to play. I thought

they wanted us to learn how to control being a werewolf. How are toy trains and stuffed animals supposed to help with that?

Eventually my guardian comes over from guarding the door to kneel next to me.

"Do you want to try putting together a puzzle?" she asks.

"No."

She picks up a partially shredded book. "I could read you a story."

"No."

"Genna, dear—"

"When do I get my things back?" I ask.

She sets the book aside and tries to take my hands in hers. I tuck them into my chest and hide them behind my upraised knees.

"I'm not sure," she says. "But they were in really bad shape."

I feel a prick behind my eyes and something else stirring inside me. "My dad got me those shoes. My mom picked out that shirt."

"It's okay," she murmurs. "You like your new clothes, don't you?"

I tug at the shirt, the sparkly horse coarse under my fingers. They're okay but—they aren't *mine*. They don't belong to me. They don't make me think of home, of Mom, of Dad, of our house, of my old friends, of riding my bike and almost running over the neighbor's cat, of hours spent hiking in the woods with my Dad, of planting flowers in the garden with Mom. They aren't mine! I tear at my shirt with a hopeless cry.

"Genna, you need to calm down."

I don't want their clothes, I don't want their toys, I don't want their food or their beds or their cages—

"Genna, *stop.*"

I scream at her, the sound changing into a wolfish snarl.

"Brad, get over here!" my guardian shouts.

The other kids stop even pretending to play with the toys as I lunge at my stupid keeper, fingers stretched out and curving into claws. She grabs my wrists as fur sprouts over me and pain wracks my body. Her face contorts as she too starts to shift into a beast. A pair of arms wrap around my middle as my arms and legs snap and change shape. I snarl and gnash my teeth, ready to rip my way free. But then more adults surround me, some human, some wolf, and they haul me out of the room just as I manage to snag that stupid book and shred it with my teeth.

I am a wolf. I am a beast filled with anger. I am a creature of survival and right now I am trapped. But despite how much I struggle, how much I snap and bite and howl, I can't free myself. There's no memory of home anymore. There's no memory of friends and family. There's only the urge to flee or fight my way to freedom. I want to *hurt* them.

My body is tossed into the Fridge and I hit the bars at the back. I scamper up onto all four paws but not fast enough. The door slams in my face and the lock slides into place, trapping me inside.

There's nothing human left in me to wonder if anyone beyond the walls of these caves can hear my howls.

December 5, 1996
Day 35

Venison stew is served as usual and we sit like obedient dogs around the circular tables in the Den. We wait hungry as Alex—our leader, our Whisper—eats his bowl of stew first. It's how things are done, is what I've been told. The alpha gets to eat first. It's a sign of respect. They didn't seem to care that I don't have any respect for him or the others, but the first time I tried eating out of turn I wasn't given any food for two days. So now I wait with the others in order to be able to eat at all.

Alex finishes his stew and when his spoon clangs in his empty dish, everyone takes it as the signal to eat their own meal. With a grudging glare at Alex who I think took his time eating, I dip my spoon and start to eat. When I realize Susan—my ever present guardian—sees me glaring, I immediately drop my gaze and focus on my bowl. I'm sick of stew. I'm sick of being here but I can't leave—not that I haven't tried.

Ten days ago I managed to slip past Susan during a bathroom break and made a run for the exit only to find guards posted there. I kept running but they were a lot faster than me. I didn't make it far. Only far enough to glimpse the thick blanket of snow, the blazing sun, feel the bone-freezing chill, smell the mix of pine trees and forest animals on the breeze. Then they caught me and I was brought back. I'm never left alone anymore.

Despite how much they talk about helping us deal with being werewolves, they sure seem more concerned about keeping us locked up. None of the adults mind. In fact, I think they like these caves hidden out of sight. They never complain and are always so patient with us kids. If I pulled half the stunts at home as I do here, my dad would have already grounded me for a week or more.

Dad. I wonder where he is. He must be looking for me. I've been gone for too long. I've been counting the days that I've been away. It's been thirty-five days. More than a month. How much longer am I going to be trapped here? How long until I can control myself so Dasc will let me leave? But I'm starting to think that we aren't meant to leave. The adults have been here forever and they don't want to leave. Have they been here since they were kids? Did they run away in the middle of the night like I did?

"Hey." James elbows me and I almost spill my spoonful of stew.

I look up and he points towards the cavern's entrance. The first person I see is Dasc and my muscles unwind. I'm so relieved to see him. Every other face in the room turns towards him too, as if they are just as glad to see him as I am. He walks a ways in before he stops and gives us a warm smile. He unzips his parka and nods to the group of teenagers behind him who I didn't notice before. They must have followed him in. They undo their parkas too and make a bee line for a nearby room. Dasc watches them until they disappear before he goes to speak with our Whisper Alex.

"Who are those people?" Rosalyn asks from the other side of the table.

"Others like us," my guardian says. It's rare for her to actually answer questions. "They've been out training with Dasc."

"Training?" I ask. "Training for what?"

Susan bows her head and returns to her food as if she doesn't hear me. I keep my eyes on the room where the new teenagers disappeared to, hoping to catch a glimpse of them again. They had been outside. I've been trying to get outside since I've been here. Why do they get to go?

We finish our meal and are ushered to the play room as usual. I sit in the corner and ignore Susan trying to get me to play as I have every other day, just like she ignores my questions. It doesn't take Susan long to stop trying and simply sit next to me, reading a book out loud as if that'll get me to listen to her. She's stubborn. So am I.

As I sit there angry and frustrated, I feel myself slowly start to unwind. I unhook my arms braced around my legs, lean back against the wall, and take a deep breath. For some reason I feel instantly better like sinking into a hot bath. I don't know why I fight against this place so much. I'm safe here. I look to Susan and listen to the story she reads about Little Red Riding Hood. It's different than I remember. In her story, the wolf saves the little girl from a terrible fire-breathing dragon pretending to be her grandmother.

"Children!"

I instantly get to my feet as I hear his voice. Dasc stands in the doorway with his arms spread wide to us. All the kids, including myself, storm over to him give him hugs. He laughs and hugs each of us. Warmth fills me up and for the first time in a long time, I'm content with where I am.

"I'm so glad to see you all," he says and kneels down so he's at our level. "How are you? Good?"

We nod and say different things at once like "I'm great!" "Good!" "I like the stew!" "We missed you!"

"I'm glad to hear it!" Dasc says and gives a hearty laugh. "All right, everyone sit down now."

We immediately take seats on the mismatched rugs and foam pads. James and I gravitate towards each other and sit while holding hands. Kelsey appears at my other side and rests his head against my shoulder. One of our guardians pulls up a chair for Dasc and he sits before us for story time. He opens up the book Susan had just been reading to me, except he tells the story with a lot more acting and excitement. He roars for the evil dragon, makes his voice small for the little girl, and puffs out his chest when he says the wolf's lines. We giggle along as he retells the story in such a funny way.

When the story is done, he closes the book and lays it across his knees.

"Yes, what a fun story. But I want you to realize something, children. Behind every story lies a seed of truth. There are monsters and there are villains in the real world. It's important for you to know where you fit in."

The laughter vanishes and we go silent, hooked on his every word. Where *do* I fit in? I want to know. I need to know and I trust Dasc to guide the way. He'll answer the scary questions for me.

"In the story, the true hero looked like a monster to those around him. Little Red Riding Hood thought he was a monster. People said he was cursed." His eyes travel over us and my heart sinks. Am I cursed? A monster? "The wolf had power—he had strength and wisdom—but power itself is not evil or wrong. He used his power for good. He made some mistakes along the way, but if he was trying to do good all along, were any of his mistakes really *bad?* Sometimes we have to make tough choices and people may see us as monsters, but that's because we are the only ones willing to do what must be done."

He leans forward and I hang on his every word.

"Remember this, children. The heroes may look like monsters, and the monsters may look like heroes. You must always be careful and learn which is which."

James raises a hand beside me so Dasc gestures for him to speak.

"Are dragons bad?" James asks.

Dasc's eyes gleam in the dim light. "Dragons are dangerous and cunning and will do everything in their power to hunt every werewolf down. That's another reason why I brought you here. I had to keep you safe from any dragons that might have found out about you."

And I believe him. Dasc has done everything he can to make us safe from outsiders and ourselves. Why do I dislike the Fridge so much? I know now that it's for my own good.

Everything the people do here is to help and protect me. I shouldn't fight them.

"Dasc?" Rosalyn says timidly.

"Yes, my dear Rosalyn?"

Her cheeks go red and she ducks her head. "Who are the older kids that came here today?"

"They've been out training to protect themselves, you, and our home. They helped me to keep the wendigos at bay and some other unsavory fiends." He waves a hand dismissively. "But let's not talk about such things. I want to see what you've all been doing!"

He gets off his chair and we rush to grab toys and bring them over to show him the games we've been playing. He sits cross-legged and listens to each one of us and even plays some imaginary games with us as well. When he wraps an arm around my shoulders, I feel safe and warm. I belong here.

We play with Dasc until one of the adults comes in and talks to him so quietly I can't hear what they're saying. His smile fades and he turns back to us with a scowl.

"I'm sorry, children, but I have to go. Duty calls. But don't worry. You're safe here and I'll be back soon."

A chorus of protests rises and I join in asking him to stay. He just smiles, waves, and quickly leaves the room. I'm sad to see him go. I feel happier when he's around.

The rest of the day we play quietly in the room, then eat the evening meal after our Whisper has his share, and wash up before lying down in our bunks. No one had an outburst today—no one was sent to the Fridge.

I curl up on my side and pull my blankets up to my chin.

I miss Dasc.

But then I ask myself—why? This morning I wanted to run away.

The warm feeling in my chest grows cold. I frown and stare at the back of James's head in the bunk next to mine. Didn't I promise James that I would get us home? Why do I suddenly want to stay? I guess these people can be nice but this isn't *home*. I don't belong here. I don't understand my own thoughts or feelings. I'm confused.

For a moment I really concentrate and clear my head.

I *don't* miss Dasc. I miss Dad. I miss Mom.

Mom, who was killed by a black wolf.

A black wolf . . .

Why have I been so blind to the black wolf right in front of me the whole time? Dasc is the black wolf. He killed my mother. *How* could I forget? How could I ever forget that? The man who killed my mom is keeping me here with these other kids. What about their parents? Did he kill them too?

I can't let myself forget. I can never forget. I run a finger down my nose as if putting on dirt like my mom used to. That's what I miss. I close my eyes and do my best to remember everything about her—her long dark hair, the smell of dirt and flowers on her skin, the way her eyes crinkled when she smiled, her laughter.

Then I remember the last words she ever said to me. No matter where I am, or what I become, she would always love me. And whenever I feel lost or afraid or alone, I need to remember that I will always have her in my heart.

I curl up on my side, knees pulled up tight to my chest, and hold my hands to my heart as if I can feel her there with me fighting back the cold and the pain and the loneliness.

My parents love me and I love them. I can't forget.

I will never forget.

But how do I get back to my family when these people don't want me to leave? They never leave me alone. They don't trust me. I'm not like Alex who gets to leave whenever he wants. I'm not like those teenagers that got to train outside. I don't want to be here and they know it.

Then it hits me.

I sit part way up and look around for any guardians nearby. The closest have fallen asleep or pace out in the hallway. Once I think the coast is clear, I prod James in the back. He flinches, grumbles, and rolls over to glare at me in the darkness.

"*What?*" he hisses at me.

I shush him and glance to the guardians. They're still asleep.

"I figured out how to get home," I whisper.

He shuffles closer until we're both leaning off the sides of our beds so our heads are almost touching.

"You know how to control the wolf?" he asks.

"No, but that's okay."

"But we can't leave until we can control it."

"I don't think we can leave even if we do."

Susan snorts and I hold my breath for what feels like a minute. When she remains asleep, I go on.

"You still want to go home, right?" I ask.

"*Of course* I do."

"Then I think we need to play pretend."

"What?"

"We have to pretend that we like it here. We have to pretend that we want to stay. Then they'll stop worrying and watching us all the time. It'll be like a game, okay? It's like when you play cops and robbers. You just pretend to be someone you're not."

"But—"

I hear footsteps come close from the hallway so I fumble in the dark to put a hand over his mouth. We remain silent until the sound fades away again.

He pries my hand off. "But we can't pretend *all* the time."

"Why not?"

"I don't know if I can! And . . . how do we know when we're actually being us?"

That's a good point. I scratch at my head and think it over.

"We'll have to make up a signal that only we know," I say. "That way, whenever we say or do something we don't mean, we'll both know it."

"What kind of signal? Should I caw like a bird?"

I punch him in the shoulder. "No, stupid. We have to do something that other people won't notice or they'll know. You get it?"

"You didn't have to punch me," he grumbles. "But what would we do then?"

What *would* we do? What would the adults not notice but we would? We couldn't be too sneaky about it because adults are good at figuring that out too. At least my parents are.

"Blink two times fast?" I suggest.

"I don't know. What about coughing?"

"That's too noisy."

"*Fine.* What do you think we should do?"

I consider it for a long time—so long that I start thinking about Mom again. What secret signal would she have used?

"I've got it," I whisper. "Whenever you're about to do something you wouldn't do, rub or scratch your nose."

"Like, pick it?"

I punch him again. "Eww! No. Just . . . run a finger from the top to the bottom of your nose or something like it's itchy."

My eyes have adjusted so I can see him nod in the darkness.

"Okay," he whispers. "I can do that. When do we start?"

"Tomorrow. Deal?"

"Deal."

"Good night, James."

"Good night, Genna."

We roll away from each other onto our mattresses and I stare up at the rough ceiling. I run my finger down my nose a few times and imagine that a beautiful woman with dark hair and the nicest smile was putting dirt on my nose.

May 14, 1997
Day 195

My name is Genna Barnes. I have been away from home for one hundred and ninety-five days. My parents are Jefferson and Andromeda Barnes. My mother was killed by a black wolf. That same black wolf is holding me captive to live with other werewolves that see him as some kind of father figure. One day I will escape with my friend James and return home.

But I haven't been that Genna for six months.

My name is Genevieve Barnes. I was turned into a werewolf over seven months ago. I ran away and was rescued by a black wolf by the name of Dasc. I owe Dasc everything. I love the other werewolves in the compound with me. I do my best to get along with everyone and learn how to control my wolf half.

At least, that's what the others think.

Everyone except James.

I swipe at my nose, pretending to have an itch, before I walk over to my guardian, Susan, and give her a big smile. James smirks at me behind her back.

"Hi, Susan!"

"Morning, dear."

I hold out my arms and she gives me a hug. We join the others at our usual table for breakfast. Susan gives me a bowl of stew and I say "Yum!" before sitting up straight with my hands in my lap waiting patiently for Alex to finish his own breakfast. While he takes his sweet time, I say good morning to everyone else at the table.

"What are we learning today?" I ask Susan. It's easy to pretend with Susan that I'm a nice little girl eager to do her studies. Susan's kind even if she's just as fooled by Dasc as the others are.

She gives me a warm smile as she braids back her dirty blonde hair. "We'll be working on your reading skills some more."

I blow out a breath. "Those books are boring now."

"I know. I think you've already read everything we have here. You're a fast learner, Genna. I'm proud of you."

I return her smile. She's proud of me. In my mind I erase her face and replace it with my mother's. Mom would be proud of me. She *had* been proud of how well I did in school. So I pretend that I'm sharing this moment with her, the person I should be sharing it with. Sometimes it's so easy to pretend. Sometimes it's hard to remember the details of Mom's face.

"When am I going to learn how to control my wolf?" I ask.

"We've been over this. It's something you have to

discover yourself. No one can teach you how to do it until you do it."

That's what she says every time and I still don't understand. How can I control it if I don't know how and no one will tell me? How am I supposed to escape if I turn into a beast that doesn't think like me, that would rather attack people than run to where I belong?

I've been doing my best to figure it out myself. I've been watching the others when they change to see if they do it differently somehow. They're able to shift into a wolf whenever they want and control themselves without anyone's help. I don't understand. And they all like it here, always helping each other and moving together in groups. No matter what I do, I can't do the same.

After breakfast, we move into the play room like every other day. Our guardians don't stick as close to us anymore. They hang out by the doors or even leave to do something else. At least, most of them du. Kelsey's guardian continues to stick to him like glue, but maybe that's because Kelsey still complains everyday about going home. He'll start crying randomly and is always so sad. I feel the same on the inside at times. I want to go home just as bad as he does but I pretend that I don't. I pretend that I love it here and the adults have begun to leave me alone more often. It's taken a long time but I've been patient. It helps that James is in on the secret and we're both playing this game. My patience has been paying off though—our plan has been working. We've even been able to walk the halls by ourselves at times. We discovered another exit we never knew about through the back of the storage area filled with barrels and crates and boxes of food and clothes. We also found a pair of guards at that exit. We can't leave yet but we're learning more every day, ready for the chance to run.

James and I sit together amongst a bunch of books spread between us. I pick them up one at a time and page through them. I've already read these stories a hundred times. There's the fairy tale of the three little pigs. Although they seem harmless, they hurt the wolf's pup so the wolf blows down their houses one by one seeking justice. I put it aside and pick up the story of Hansel and Gretel where a witch with magical powers kills their parents but a werewolf gives them its gift so they are able to defeat the witch in the end. I want to throw the book but I pretend to enjoy it as the guardian at the door watches us.

None of the stories are how I remember them from when Mom or Dad would read them to me as I sat snuggled up in bed. But as I read these stories over and over again, I've begun to forget how the stories actually went. What did happen to the three little pigs? Why did the wolf go after them? Was there a dragon in the story of little red riding hood? Was there even a wolf in the story of Hansel and Gretel? I don't remember.

I pick over the books, not caring to read any of them. James flips the pages aimlessly beside me, his chin propped up in his hand.

"I wish they had books on how to survive out there," James mutters out of the side of his mouth.

"Me too," I whisper.

Someone comes up behind us and I tilt my face up to find Rosalyn standing there with her hands on her hips.

"Are you done with this?" she demands. She's gotten super bossy.

"Why don't you ask nicely?" I say.

She scowls at me and tries to snatch the book out of my hands but I'm too quick for her and hold it out of reach on my other side. I don't care to keep it but Rosalyn is always so rude to me that I do it just to make her angry.

"You've read it a thousand times!" she whines and throws her body against my back with her arms straining towards the book. I hold it out even farther but her weight knocks me down to the floor.

She starts clawing at my hair so I dig my elbow into her side. We get into a heated tussle, pulling each other's hair, pushing against each other's face, and kicking our legs.

"Stoooooop," James groans beside us but doesn't move to interfere.

Rosalyn shrieks when I jab a finger into her cheek and she slaps me across the face, the book all but forgotten now.

"No one likes you!" she yells and grabs a fistful of my hair.

I place both hands on her throat and push hard. "Too bad you don't have your gentle giant here to protect you!"

She sucks in a sharp breath, her eyes go wide, and then she starts furiously punching me everywhere she can reach. I curl up with my arms to protect me while I kick out with one leg trying to keep her back.

"That's enough, you two!" Susan wraps her arms around Rosalyn's middle and pulls her off me while someone else drags me backwards from behind.

We're both set forcefully down as we pant and catch our breath. Rosalyn's face is red and her lower lip trembles as she starts to silently cry. Every time anyone brings up her "gentle giant"—her brother—she cries like a baby. It's a button I've pressed more than a few times. Despite how much she talks about liking it here, she always turns on the waterworks whenever she thinks about her brother. A part of her still wants to go home just as much as I do.

"What on earth were you two fighting about?" Susan says and finally lets go of Rosalyn.

"She wouldn't give me that book!" Rosalyn shouts and jabs a finger at the thing lying in a heap on the ground, some of the pages ripped.

"Like you can even read," I snap.

She curls her fists and puffs up, her face going even more brightly red. "I can read!"

Susan holds her hands out between us. "Children, that's enough—"

"You're so stupid!" I shout back and can feel my arms shaking. I don't care if I'm supposed to pretend I like it here or behave. I'm *angry*. Stupid Rosalyn wants to stay here and make Dasc think she's *so* smart because she's read all the books when I only want to choke him. "I bet your mom is glad you're gone!"

"I'm glad your mom is *dead*!"

My hold snaps like a twig. Fur spurts all over my body and I hardly feel the pain of it as my limbs twist into a different shape. I don't hear what any of the adults are shouting at me as I lunge for Rosalyn. My jaws open wide and I'm ready to rip her to pieces. Another furry body collides with mine and we roll away into the wall. Sharp smells and sounds bombard me and I'm a spitting, snarling beast on all fours. I see threats everywhere and my hackles rise. My head whips around to the door and I sprint towards it before the adults can pin me down. I get partway down the hallway before I'm flattened by a pile of bodies on top of mine. I writhe and snap my teeth and kick furiously to escape. My claws scratch their faces and muzzles, my teeth clamp onto their fur, my vicious snarls drown out their whines and howls.

I need to attack. I need to show them my anger. I need to avenge my pack!

My pack.

My family.

Family . . . Mom. Dad.

A shudder travels through me and the weight of the others pins me down so I can't move. I stop fighting and eventually they pick me up and carry me to the Fridge where I'm locked away. The ferocity in me breaks into tiny pieces. I don't gnaw on the bars. I don't dig into the floor. I don't bark or howl. Anger and agitation don't take over my mind like usual. Instead of the deranged beast I've always been before, I pace a circle until I curl up into a ball at the back of my cage and rest my head on my forelegs.

All the nasty things I want to do—they just become thoughts. I don't feel like I have to do them, not like the other times I've shifted. I still think about bashing my way out of this cage but I know I can't.

The only thing I can think about is Mom and a steady whine escapes me.

No matter where you are, no matter what you become, I will always love you.

I've repeated the words to myself a thousand times to make sure I never forget them. I may feel alone here but I realize I'm not alone, not really. Somewhere else in the world, my dad is still out there looking for me. That's where I belong. That's my pack.

I am a wolf. I am a nightmare of teeth and claws. But I am not alone.

And no matter where I am, no matter what I become, my family will always love me.

The urge to bite everyone in sight fades away. I run a paw down the length of my muzzle and over my snout.

I am not alone.

Repeating those words over and over again in my head, my mind feels clearer than it has in a long time. I look down at my paws and for the first time I really see myself. I flex my toes and watch how the claws make the smallest grooves in the dirt. I shift my tail, natural and familiar as if it's always been there. My shiny black fur catches the light and I study the soft tips, the bluish tint, the waves. They are all a part of me. Sure, there's anger beneath that I never felt before I became this but it's like a part of me that's just been made worse. Instead of wanting to yell at Rosalyn like I would have before becoming a werewolf, I wanted to hurt her. But this is me now.

I know from my dad that there is no changing what I've become. I am and always will be a wolf. I can't change who or what I am—but maybe I can change what happens next.

I am a wolf.

The world changes around me as I accept that. I blink a few times and see everything around me clearly. Susan and others lay around the outside of the bars, most already dozing off. But Susan watches me intently in a way she never has before. I tilt my head slowly this way and that as

I'm mesmerized by the way the light changes the color of her fur from golden brown to brilliant sunshine. It's not the only thing I've never noticed before. The smallest sounds capture my attention but they don't overwhelm me—the whisper of wind through gaps in the tunnels, the sprinkle of loose dirt falling from the ceiling, the steady breaths of the wolves around me. Being a wolf isn't a jumble of sensations and surge of anger anymore. Somehow I've done the impossible. Somehow . . . somehow I think I'm in control of myself.

Despite that, even though I keep my head, Susan and the others don't let me out. Tired and still taking in everything around me, I settle in with my head on my paws. My ears twitch as I catch new noises and try to make them out.

It feels like hours in the Fridge before I hear soft footsteps approaching. I lift my head to see Dasc enter the room. He walks upright as a human with his hands tucked into his pockets. As usual, I'm filled with a sense of calm and relief when I see him. He is the alpha here. He will protect us.

Susan rises and he lays a hand on her furry head. She gives a low bow as she shifts at will back into her own human form. Once she's lost her fur, she stands and talks quietly to Dasc but I can still hear their every word.

"She got into a fight with Rosalyn over a book," Susan says.

"She's calm," he says and his gaze remains on me. I stare back. "Those are human eyes."

"Yes, I believe she's safe now."

He rocks back on his heels and cocks his head. "That's one of the fastest assimilations I've seen."

Susan glances over her shoulder at me. "She's a very special girl."

"I know."

He moves around her and comes within a foot from the bars of my cage. He slowly sinks down into a crouch before me. A warm smile spreads on his face and there's a glimmer in his eyes.

"Genevieve, I want you to try something for me," he says. "Shift back."

I blink and let out a wolfish huff. How do I shift back? I don't have a clue how I've managed to do it before.

He chuckles. "I have faith in you. I know you can do it."

Somehow I believe it too when he says it. So I stare at my paws and try to imagine my hands there instead. I'm not sure if that's supposed to work but I soon realize it's not as I remain a black wolf. I look to Dasc for help but he just nods.

A steady whine escapes me as I keep trying but nothing happens. I give a sharp bark in my frustration.

"Now, now, no need to get so worked up" Dasc says and presses a finger to his lips. "You discovered your way to this point. You discovered the pack. Now you need to discover yourself again."

I discovered the pack. Is that the answer to the problem of being a werewolf? Is that really all it took? There must be more to it. But Dasc is right. He's always right. And if he believes I can do this, then I can.

I have to discover myself. Who am I?

My name is Genevieve Barnes. I have been a werewolf for over seven months. I ran away from home and was taken in by Dasc. I am a wolf but I am also a girl. My parents are Jefferson and Andromeda Barnes. Like my father, I try to protect the people around me. I will do my best to protect James. I will do whatever it takes to save us both.

I am the girl who does not fear. I am the girl who will be feared.

That is who I am.

The fur on my paws shrinks away and pain overtakes me as I change my shape from wolf to human. My fingers curl into the dirt beneath me and I pant as I catch my breath. I did it. I can't believe I did it.

Dasc wraps both hands around the bars in front of me and gives me his biggest smile yet.

"That's my girl."

April 30, 2000
Day 1,277

The face I show to the others is a mask made of iron. No one suspects anything about me. I'm the fierce girl. I am cold as ice. I am tough as steel. The girl beneath isn't much different except for one key difference—she doesn't belong here. She has no love for this place. And one day, she will be free.

But there are some days when even my mask is tested.

James crouches in the mud at my feet wiping blood from the corner of his mouth. I stand over him with fists raised and legs slightly bent. Our instructor circles around us in this mucky field not far from the underground compound. The rest of our class stands around with bruises, split lips, black eyes, and scrapes. A few wisps of my long hair float in front of my face and my knuckles are scuffed, but I've fared better than any of the others. Rosalyn glares at me from behind our instructor's back with her arms crossed.

"Get up," Ryan snaps and continues to circle us.

James struggles up, pushing off from his knees until he stands facing me once again. He slowly brings his fists up covered in mud and bits of grass.

"Again."

He lunges forward, stepping into his punch, but I slip past him. Well, mostly. I let his knuckles graze my shoulder as an act of kindness for my friend. I don't like hitting him and if James can't fight properly, Ryan will make me be merciless—or worse, he'll step in to be James's opponent.

Ryan circles around behind me and kicks out the back of my leg. I fall to one knee in the mud with a grunt.

"You let him get that shot," he says.

Without comment, I rise back into my stance.

"Again."

This time when James punches, I dodge and return with a jab to his ribs. He huffs but manages to sucker punch me in the ear. We stumble away from each other.

"Again!" Ryan barks at us.

We clash again, friend against friend, each scoring hits and earning bruises. When I hook his leg and send him into the mud once more, Ryan comes over to click his tongue.

"You need to be stronger. You need to be faster. If we are weak, we will not survive." He turns to the crowd behind him. "Children, what do we say?"

"If one falls, the pack survives," they chant in unison. "If there is rot, we cut it out. The pack survives."

"You're rotting, James," our instructor leers. "The pack can't survive if it has to coddle the weaklings. You understand don't you?"

James nods and pants as he struggles upright.

But then Ryan looks to me and I know what he wants me to do. The Genna he knows doesn't hesitate to follow orders. The girl wearing my face would beat James mercilessly for being today's failure. But the girl I am at heart, the one still struggling to be free, looks down at James with pity and concern. I don't want to hurt him. He doesn't deserve to be beaten for failing to best me. What does it prove? What does any of this prove?

So I hesitate. James looks up and holds my gaze. He knows. I know. We both know if I don't do anything, then Ryan will hurt him much worse.

My mask can't fail if we ever want to make it home.

I kick James in the ribs and he falls backwards into the mud. I kick him two more times, straighten, and look to Ryan for approval. He dips his head.

"Let the pain be a reminder," Ryan says. "If you were fighting someone other than a comrade, you'd be dead. The pain is insignificant to that. We do this to make you stronger. We care about you. Do you understand?"

James nods weakly.

"Get up on your own."

I fight the impulse to reach out and help my friend to his feet. Instead, I clench my hands into fists at my sides and watch as James pushes off from the ground, puts one foot under him, and then the other. When he finally stands, he presses a hand to his ribs with a grimace. Ryan pats him on the shoulder as if he really is concerned about James. If Ryan really cared, he wouldn't force us to attack each other.

"You'll heal quickly," Ryan says as if that makes it better. He pats me on the shoulder too. I don't flinch or throw him off. I don't make any move whatsoever. I remain fierce. I remain cold.

"Time for a puzzle," he says and claps his hands together. "Boys are the map makers today. Girls are the scouts. We'll start at the Werewood. Go."

As a group we shift into our other half. For some it's still a real struggle to control the transformation. I change into it easily as if throwing on a jacket. I've accepted this part of myself and where I belong. I'm not a part of this pack but I know the pack that claims me. My family back home. It grounds me, let's me sniff at the air and trot around not as a wild animal bent on anger and destruction but as myself with more fur. There's power in my limbs, in my strong jaws, in my sharp eyes and sensitive ears. There's a hunger too and an itch at the top of my spine that tells me I need to bite something. I've accepted those parts of myself too. I know what I am, but I've also made the decision that the only person who can truly make me a monster is myself.

Ryan, now a dusty colored timber wolf, barks at us and starts to run away. We follow close behind in a loose group, the faster of us racing to beat the others. I run near the front of the pack as usual and Rosalyn nips at my heels. She's been trying to outdo me since we got here. She's also mean to James and me so I make sure it's a real challenge for her. Her frustration gives me some happiness.

We reach a section of the woods with great, gnarled trees. Their twisted limbs look like black snakes wrapped around each other and glisten with morning dew. The Werewood.

Ryan barks again and the boys separate from the pack to surround him. One more bark and us girls take a seat to wait for our side of the task. The boys hurry off into the Werewood to set up the game. We've been doing this for a few months now to test our memory and survival skills. I take this as an opportunity to sit and stare off in the opposite direction towards the south. Nose held high, I take in what scents come to me. Somewhere far away down there is home. Somewhere out there is my father. Each morning before I get out of bed, I think of his face and try to remember everything about him and Mom. I picture home—the cabin and barn, the flower beds, my pink bike, the neighbor's cat, everything I can think of. But what I can remember becomes a little less each day. Was the cat black or a tabby? Did my bike have a basket or not? Worst of all, it becomes harder to picture exactly what my parents look like. I can't forget. I can't.

But there's still one thing I will never forget. How my mom died and who killed her.

I blink and look to the girls spread out on the forest floor. Rosalyn sticks out with her silver coat and black face. I catch her staring at me but she quickly looks away. No one looks off towards their homes, no one tries to run away even though we're outside and currently without supervision. I thought they couldn't be so stupid to leave us alone but we're not truly alone. I've discovered there is a constant ring of guards surrounding the compound. No one comes or goes without the adults knowing. Little Kelsey tried a few months ago. He made it a mile before they caught him and hauled him back. They haven't let him out anywhere without an adult ever since.

The forest stretches on for miles around us quiet and seemingly empty. It's almost cruel. I'd like to think that I could take off right now and they'd never catch me but they always do. Yet I still believe there has to be a way to escape. I can't stop believing that. I won't.

I pick up Ryan's scent before I see him. He barks at us and we rise to follow. He leads us a ways through the trees before we stop in front of markings scratched in the dirt. The scent of the boys has been left behind like an echo of them. Ryan points with one paw to the markings, barks once more, and trots away. It had been a surprise the first time he did this. If we don't manage to follow the clues left by the boys and make it back to the compound, they won't bother guiding us back. We have to make it on our own. Of course, if we wander too far in the wrong direction—like south to home—they'll catch us. We have to follow their rules, even if their rules are dumb.

Letting out a huff, I study the marks in the dirt. There's a triangle, two lines, and a twig above it. That means…they went south and the next sign will be at a tree. I'd rather just follow their scents but they lead in every which direction to confuse us. We have to follow the signs.

I hold out a paw towards the south and several of the others do the same. We bark in agreement and head off at a trot. We find the next clue not too far away beneath a big maple. One after another, we find the messages left behind by the boys and work our way through the woods. We're generally in agreement about what the signs mean but when we do come to a disagreement, we go by a majority vote of paws pointing in the direction of where to go.

Then we come to a sign that's poorly marked and slightly smudged as if one of the boys wasn't paying attention when they quickly left the area and stepped through it. I think we should go east but Rosalyn keeps barking and pointing west. The others start barking too and we get to the point we're snarling at each other. I remain adamant that I'm right but Rosalyn refuses to back down. We get real close and bare our teeth in each other's face, spit flying and hackles rising. Then Rosalyn swipes a paw at my face. I dodge but by the time I look back, she's already turned tail and started running in the direction she's decided we should go.

Before anyone's dumb enough to follow after her, I snap my teeth at the others and paw at the ground, making it clear they are to stay put. Then I chase after Rosalyn. I'll drag her stupid hide back if I have to.

She's a blur between the trees but I'm faster. I've always been better than her but she's too stupid to accept it. Once she realizes I'm behind her and closing fast, she yips and kicks it up a notch. At this point she's not even looking for another clue; she's just trying to run away from me. I bark at her back but she keeps on going. Soon we're out of the Werewood and quickly moving into unknown territory.

Then I realize we haven't come across any of the adults in a while. I haven't see any of the guards that keep watch to make sure we don't run away. I start to slow as I consider it and sniff at the air for signs of any others nearby. My paws stumble to a halt and I face south once again. Could I make it this time? Am I far enough away that they couldn't catch me? But there could still be someone watching and if I ran now, they'd never let me out of their sight again.

I stand there shifting from paw to paw, unable to decide to risk it or not. I want to go so badly but I'm afraid I'll be caught. Every game I've been playing would be for nothing if I don't actually manage to escape.

A breeze tickles my nose and with it comes a foul stench. I know what dead animals smell like. Enough have been brought in for meals that I know that odor. But this…this is something decayed and rotten. My ears swivel listening for any sound of danger as my fur stands on end. This smell is *wrong*. I inch silently beneath the trees looking this way and that as I follow the smell. But then I come across another scent—death.

Keeping low to the ground, I continue on until I find two of the adults—some of the guards—lying dead. Their fur is matted with blood and their sides ripped open in a horrible display. I freeze and hunch even lower to the ground, wishing I could make myself invisible. The rotten smell hangs about the two bodies. I think it's from whatever killed these two. I need to get out of here.

But then it hits me. The guards are dead. There won't be anyone watching if I run right now. My head points south again like a compass leading me home. I could leave. I could be free. I don't care if there's something dangerous out in the woods. I'm fast and small. I could out run whatever it is or hide where it can't find me. I could make it.

I could go home.

A bone-chilling shriek splits the silence. I automatically

pivot towards the sound before flattening to the ground. It's a wolf in pain or fear.

Rosalyn.

My eyes turn south again. Home. It's out there. I just have to run for it.

A high-pitched scream like a rabbit dying sends my heart hammering. Whatever monster Rosalyn has come across is killing her. I can smell the blood from here. It's a horrible thing to hear and sends shivers down my spine. She's in trouble and I'm right here—but so is a chance at freedom.

What would Dad do?

I face west and run.

The smell of decaying things fills my nostrils and I pant heavily as I sprint for where Rosalyn's cries of pain echo. Between the trees, two freakishly skinny and tall figures loom. Their skin is bone-white and they wear tattered clothes that hang in scraps around their waist. Rosalyn lays at their feet as they hover over her, their fingers extended into spiky claws. I run headlong towards them with teeth bared and a snarl ripping out of my throat. One turns to face me—it's like looking into the face of a skeleton with terrifying black eyes. Its mouth opens to expose cracked and jagged teeth.

I leap for its throat.

In a flash of searing pain, I find its claws ripping across my face and throwing me to the side. With a yelp, I hit the forest floor hard. I scramble back to my feet and whip around to face the thin monsters and their wicked claws. Blood mingles with their scent from myself and Rosalyn behind them. Her silver fur is stained red and she tries to inch away, dragging herself by her forelegs.

In a dangerous gambit I rush at the creatures' legs. I manage to make one tumble to the side but the other sidesteps me. Spinning back around, I put myself between Rosalyn and the nightmares before me. I snap my teeth, lower my head, expose my fangs, and flatten my ears. When they try to move towards me, I bite at their hands and feet in a vicious frenzy. But I can't keep my eyes on both of them. When I lunge at one, the other moves around behind me. Long claws jab at my back and slice at my legs. My canines draw blood but it's not enough. I yelp as those terrible hands wrap around my middle and the claws dig into my gut. A breathless whine escapes me as I struggle to free myself. I'm lifted up higher and higher until I can feel the monster's breath on my neck. It sinks its teeth into my exposed throat.

Suddenly, I'm ripped away from the thing and tumble to the ground as it gives a terrible cry of its own. In a fog of pain, I lift my head to find someone else amongst the creatures. Susan shifts on her feet as her human self with a small, shiny blade in her hand. Her blonde hair flies loose as she whirls around the creepy things and slashes with her blade. Trembling and in great pain, I can only watch as she takes the pair on. They leave cuts across her arms and her face but she makes no sound as she returns the favor. She ducks and swivels on her feet and manages to come up directly behind one to plunge her little blade into its back. I flatten my ears against the noise it makes.

It crumples to the ground and only one creature remains. Susan turns about on it, her blade flashing in her deadly hands. Its black eyes narrow, it looses a hiss between its foul teeth, and then sprints into the woods so fast it's a blur. Susan takes two steps after it but then halts. Her eyes shift to me.

"*Genna*," she rasps and kneels on the bloody ground next to Rosalyn and me. "Don't move. You'll make it worse. Just hold on."

She plants her hands on the ground while I struggle to breathe and she transforms. Her howls echo through the woods on and on until others join her in the distance. The howls continue and grow louder as the others come closer. A steady whine escapes between my tightly clenched teeth and I lay on the ground unmoving curled in on myself. Before me, Rosalyn's chest barely moves up and down as she takes in ragged breaths.

The howls eventually change into voices. The rest of the pack has found us.

"Quickly, help me," Susan says.

While a group of adults carefully lift Rosalyn up between them, Susan picks me up in her arms alone. She strains at my weight but carries me off beneath the trees. My paws shake and everything hurts but I feel safe in her embrace. There's strength in her now that I did not see before. She saved us. She doesn't tell me it'll be okay or that everything will be all right. She just tells me to hold on, that I'm strong enough to survive this. For some reason, it makes me feel better.

When we reach the compound, we're immediately surrounded by the rest of the pack. They rush us inside and everything becomes a blur of bodies and worried voices. Susan stays with me and helps clean the cuts. I yelp and whine but she tells me to hold still so I do. At long last, when the stitches are done and they've put honey over them, I'm allowed to rest. Susan brings me water and kneels by my head to gently smooth the fur over my head.

"You were brave out there," she says quietly. "You saved Rosalyn's life. Wait a few days until you shift. You'll heal better that way."

I give a gentle huff to let her know I understand.

Then I feel it—the familiar sensation that everything is right in the world and my nerves are soothed. It becomes easier to ignore the pain as if it doesn't even exist. A shadow falls over me.

"What happened?"

It's Dasc.

Susan rises and I don't even bother to tilt my head to watch them talk.

"Wendigos," Susan whispers. "They killed Evie and Fred while they were on patrol. The girls came across them during their training."

"How many of them?" His voice sounds tight.

"Two. I killed one. The other got away."

He sighs and they're silent for a long time as my eyelids begin to close. I'm so tired.

"And the girls?" Dasc asks eventually.

"Rosalyn was practically eviscerated. It'll take a long time for her to heal but she should make it. Genna got hurt pretty badly defending her but she fared better. They'll be okay."

"You make sure they get whatever they need. I'll be back."

"Of course," Susan says and returns to her spot on the floor next to me.

I fall asleep with Susan's hand resting on my head. Sometime in the night when the only light is from a candle on the far side of the room, I wake. Susan's still beside me with a blanket over her legs and her head against the wall sitting propped up as she sleeps. The copper tang of blood hits my senses and I lift my head to find Dasc standing in the doorway of the small room.

When he raises a finger to press it to his lips in a motion to keep me silent, blood drips from his hand. In fact, both hands are covered in dark blood and it's splattered across his face. I should be frightened by such a sight but I'm not.

"Go back to sleep," he whispers. "It's okay. There are no bad monsters left to find you in the darkness." He turns about to leave but then pauses and looks at me over his shoulder. His eyes glint in the flickering light of the candle. "The good monsters are here to keep you safe."

As if the words are exactly what I need to hear, my eyes close once more and I fall into a dreamless sleep. When I wake again, I find Susan and our Whisper looking at the deep gouges and punctures in my side. It hurts to breathe, much less move, so I lay there motionless drifting in and out of a sleep for the next few days. Every time I wake, Susan is there taking care of me. She brings in more blankets for the both of us, makes sure I have soup to eat and water to drink. She carefully applies honey over my stitches and gently strokes my fur.

Bits of my mask of iron chip away because I'm not play pretending anymore when I realize I care for Susan too. I stretch out a paw and she holds it in her hands as we both fall asleep once again, my head in her lap.

The next morning Susan's there as Dasc returns to

announce that I am well enough to shift back to my human self. Susan keeps a hand on my shoulder as I pass through the agonizing change and come out the other side panting as a girl once again. With Susan at my side, I finally walk out of that room on my own two feet.

The second I'm outside the door, James rushes up to me. "Genna!"

He goes for a hug but Susan snaps out her hand to keep him back. "She's not well enough yet."

James ducks his head and his cheeks turn red. I reach out and take his hand to make him—and myself—feel better.

"I waited outside your door the whole time," he says. "They wouldn't let me in."

"She needed to rest," Susan says.

I squeeze my friend's hand. "I'm okay."

"If you say so."

"I do say so."

Susan puts some pressure on my shoulder to keep me moving. "We should get you some breakfast."

"I want to see Rosalyn."

She blinks and stares. "She's still resting. She was hurt worse than you were."

"I want to see her."

"Child—"

Dasc suddenly appears behind us. "She can come with me. I'll take her."

In an instant Susan moves away and Dasc takes her place with his hand on my shoulder. He gives me a wide smile and I can feel the warmth of his attention.

"Follow me," he says.

We leave Susan and James behind as we head slowly to Rosalyn's room. It hurts to move too fast and he seems to know it. After a short walk down the hallway, we come to another room with a closed door. He opens the way for us and I find Rosalyn as a wolf lying on a bed of blankets like the one I just left. Her own guardian—Mathias—sits on the floor beside her head. Her middle is wrapped round and round and she looks terrible. When she realizes we've entered the room, her eyes stare glumly at me.

We've never been friends, but seeing her like this…

I limp to her side and ever so carefully sit beside her so I can lay a hand on her shoulder. She continues to watch me with deadened eyes and lets out a soft whine. Her pain echoes in my own chest. We may not be friends but we're part of the same pack.

I clench my jaw and look to Dasc. "Did you kill it? The wendigo?"

The blue of his eyes catches the light from the candles and it's as if the flames are dancing within them. "Yes." He looks over Rosalyn and the light vanishes from his face, his blue eyes flashing golden. "I was not quick and I was not kind."

I remember the blood on his hands when he returned. I don't want to think about what he did but part of me wishes I had been there.

"Good," I say.

I sit with Rosalyn a while longer, a little more of my mask breaking away as the real me decides there's more monster to me than I thought.

And I'm not ashamed one bit.

August 13, 2004
Day 2,843

When I dodge a spout of water pretending it to be acid and manage to deflect the rock thrown with my shield, I get a rare smile from our Whisper.

"Well done, Genna," he says as he juggles a small stone in his hand. He's been chucking rocks at us for the last half hour.

"Thanks, Alex," I say with a respectful nod.

His gaze travels to the others around me—James, Rosalyn, Kelsey, and the rest—with shields of their own. "Now if only the *rest* of you could manage to dodge the attacks of our hypothetical hydra, we might be able to finish this training session before nightfall. Again!"

I bend my knees and position my shield before me with eyes peeking over the top rim. Alex, Susan, and a large group of our mentors prepare water guns and rocks once more. We've been getting drilled on hydra combat for the past week. In the weeks before that, it was vampires, before that wendigos, and trolls and so on. They're preparing us for the dangers out there but I keep getting the feeling there's more to it all, something they haven't told us yet.

I've thrown myself whole-heartedly into the training. The danger is real—Rosalyn and I know that better than anyone. The most dangerous things the others have come across in their excursions have been random trolls or the lone vampire quickly trying to make it out of our territory once they've realized their mistake. This area is ours and we've made our claim clear. A wendigo hasn't been spotted within a hundred miles of the compound since the day Rosalyn and I came across that pair. Dasc made sure to send a message to the others. They won't bother us again.

But the dangers I've learned about and trained to fight have only reminded me what a big world this is and how far away I am from my father. He works as an IMS agent. He faces these things every day. For all I know, a monster could have killed him by now and I would have no way of knowing. I've been granted more freedom, that's for sure, but the timing has never been right to make my escape with James. And if I'm being honest with myself, I don't want to go. Not yet. The people here…they aren't Dasc. They're good at heart and care about each other. How can I simply leave them behind to be instruments of Dasc's schemes? I can't let myself forget that I wasn't the only one taken from home. Every single one of them was brought here by some strange calling that could only have been from Dasc. Why did he take us? Was he truly that lonely? Or is there more to the story as I suspect?

If any of the others feel the same way I do, they haven't
let on for years. Kelsey has given up completely on getting
away from this place and the others act the same way. It's
only in late night whispered conversations that James and I
futilely discuss plans to free ourselves and the others. But
there are times when I doubt myself and my purpose. What
would be waiting for me if I went back? Would the people
hate me like I've been told a thousand times by the others?
Would I be subjected to the terrible serum I've heard about
that would tear me apart from the inside meant to make
werewolves docile slaves?

Are we safer here after all?

A rock almost smacks me in the side of the head and I
leave my thoughts of doubt behind as I focus on training
once again.

We're worked into the night until Alex is satisfied with
our progress for the day. Drenched in sweat, we break off to
clean up in the tubs before gathering again for supper. We
chat amongst ourselves as Alex eats his meal first. Once his
spoon hits the table, the rest of us automatically begin
eating our own food. Night draws in and we do our usual
chores—cleaning up the main area, tossing out the filthy
water from washing dishes, and sweeping the floors. While
Kelsey and a few others head out for night patrol, the rest of
us head for bed. We've moved into a larger chamber to be
able to fit us. We don't keep separate rooms here. It's better
to always be together as a pack. The lone wolf flounders.
The pack survives.

Once the lights are out and I hear the others fall asleep,
I tug out my little slip of fabric and stare at it in the dark
even though I can't read the words on it. It's just to remind

myself where I come from and where I have to get back to someday. That little bit of fabric is precious to me and I've done everything to make sure it stays secret. No one else knows I have it except for James, and I plan on keeping it that way. I tuck it back into its hiding spot in the sole of my shoe before settling in to fall asleep.

Sometime in the night I'm prodded urgently in the shoulder. I jerk awake and find Dasc leaning over me. He's also woken up James. His dark silhouette motions for us to follow him. What's going on?

As soon as we're out of the room and in the hallway, Dasc draws us close to him.

"We have a problem," he says quietly. "Get dressed and meet me at the southern tunnel exit immediately. Go."

James and I exchange a look before hustling back into the big chamber to get dressed in the dark. When we return to the hallway, Dasc is already gone.

"What do you think's going on?" James whispers as we jog through the tunnels.

"No idea. Makes me nervous."

When we finally reach the southern exit, we find not only Dasc waiting there but also Alex, Kelsey's mentor Brad, and Susan. The adults are talking quietly amongst themselves and shouldering backpacks. Once we're spotted, their conversation stops. Dasc waves us forward to join their gathering.

"What's going on?" I ask.

Susan lays a hand on my shoulder. "It's Kelsey. He's run away."

Part of me thinks "good for him." The other part worries sick about him on his own out there in the wilderness. He's in real danger. He's not a very good fighter and he's small for his age. I know what lurks out there. If he doesn't manage to find help soon . . . we'll have to rescue him.

"Why do you need us?" James asks.

Dasc clasps his hands behind his back. "Because you two are probably the closest friends he has. He doesn't understand the danger he's running into. I want you two to accompany us to help persuade him to come home."

Instinctively I want to swallow but I purposefully make no motion of any kind. I've had practice and patience on my side for a long time to be able to pull it off. I'll never give myself away. We're going to be passing the boundaries of werewolf territory and I'll be the closest I've ever been to home. My chest aches as I consider what that means. Dasc is going to be there but perhaps by some miracle we could . . . maybe we can . . .

No. I can't raise my hopes like that despite how much I'd like to. There's no way to plan for the circumstances ahead of us. A decision can only be made in the moment but I'll be prepared for the opportunity should it arise.

And then there's the other thing. I've been paying close attention to Dasc and figuring out how he works. If Dasc really wanted to persuade Kelsey to come back, he could just *compel* Kelsey to come back. I haven't failed to notice the effect he has on us when he's around. James and I aren't needed for this, so maybe this isn't just about Kelsey but about us as well. What if Dasc has figured us out? We'll need to be extra careful.

"I hope you're ready for a long midnight run," he says and rubs his hands together as if excited at the prospect.

"Will you join me?" James and I nod in unison. "Then we better get moving."

"Good luck," Alex says. "I'll keep an eye on things as usual."

"There's a good lad."

Alex steps out of the way as Dasc sinks to the floor to shift. He does it so fast, it's like he morphs in the second between standing as a human and then on all fours as a wolf. As seamless as breathing. Susan and Brad change next with more contorting and grimacing. James and I follow suit not far behind. My senses hone in on the pack around me—my comrades. There's a bond between us that ties us together and feels oddly natural and comforting.

At Dasc's signal, we move out of the exit, past the guards stationed outside, and into the darkness of the forest beyond. Though there is little light, my wolfish eyes can see far more than Genna the girl can. My footfalls do not falter or stumble. I am stealth and speed. I am a shadow in the night. I am a wolf.

The five of us run on through the night following Kelsey's scent through the forest. Dasc is always so sure of where he's going, and even when the trail is almost too faint for me, he can still track it. We hardly take any breaks to rest because from the weakening scent of Kelsey's trail it doesn't seem like he's stopping either. He's made a full on run for it. I understand. If I tasted freedom like that, I'd be running as fast as I could too. But…would I? Could I really just leave the rest of them behind to the seclusion of Dasc's compound tucked away in the boreal forest of Canada? Never to see their families again? Could I be so selfish?

By the time the sun rises, we still haven't found Kelsey. I'm tired, James is tired beside me, and the others are flagging. Well, that is, everyone except for Dasc. As werewolves, the magic in our blood helps us heal faster than humans and makes runs like this possible. But Dasc is on another level entirely. I analyze that little detail and tuck it into the back of my mind for later consideration. I've been doing my best to catalog every tidbit about him that I can. He's been using his compulsion less and less on me—I can feel it—so it makes it easier to see the flaws, the abilities, the quirks that I might otherwise have ignored if he wanted me to see him blindly on a pedestal like everyone else does.

When Dasc brings us to an abrupt halt on the edge of a paved road, I have my first true look at civilization beyond the confines of the compound since I was seven. A roadway with yellow and white lines. It's so simple and yet it's like being smacked in the face by the familiar and distant past. It's a jarring reminder that the world is not made solely up of forests and underground tunnels. There's a whole world out there with people living normal lives and doing . . . whatever it is normal people do. I don't even know anymore. My life has been combat training, obedience, and a yearning to escape since I was seven.

That's when it hits me. I've been at that compound longer than I had lived with my parents. All the time that's been stripped away from me rattles anger deep in my bones and it's hard to stop the hackles from rising on my back. The monster beside me took those seven years and then some away from me. The time in the compound wasn't my life—it was his stolen time.

Dasc shifts as he walks out into the middle of the road and looks both ways. He gestures to us to do the same. Right now I don't want to do a thing he says. I want to run. I'm still a wolf. I could book it, but I know how fast he can shift and he has more energy than I do. I'm tired and my paws ache. Trying to flee now wouldn't work and I know it. So I shift along with the others.

"The trail ends here," Dasc announces and plants his hands on his waist. "He must have hitchhiked."

"How on earth are we supposed to find him then?" Brad says heavily and his shoulders sag. This is probably the first time he's shown any kind of concern about Kelsey despite being his mentor and guardian. I think he despises being assigned to the most stubborn child of our generation that refused to let go of the thought of returning home. Then I realize Brad's concern is more about himself as he eyes Dasc warily like he's going to be in trouble for Kelsey managing to escape.

I can only hope Kelsey gets as far away from this place as fast as he can.

"I think I know where he'll be heading," Dasc says. "But I'll need to make a few phone calls. We won't be able to get any service until about a day's run southwest. We'll rest up for a few hours and move out again."

"But the longer we stay here, the further he gets away," Brad argues.

Quick as a flash, Dasc's eyes flare golden and he bares his teeth that lengthen into wolf canines. "Maybe if you saw to it that he didn't run away, we wouldn't be in this position."

Brad bows and back pedals away from our alpha. I stand still and keep my eyes on Dasc despite not wanting to draw his wrath upon me next. It's instinctual for me to show that I'm not afraid. Dasc meets my gaze and his teeth and eyes revert back to normal.

"We're all tired and I doubt we'll be able to catch up to him if he's hitched a ride," he says calmly. "The best we can do now is rest and then get into phone service so I can call my contacts, see if they can reach Kelsey before he gets into trouble. I'll take first watch."

He waves us on across the road and we settle down in a grove of spruces, shifting back into wolf form in case anyone comes across us by accident. Then they'll only see a pack of wolves, not a group of odd strangers hiding in the forest. After a few hours' sleep, when the sun has risen in the sky and we've had a scant breakfast, we head out once again. It's a long trek, wherever we're headed, and we don't reach our destination until after nightfall.

If I thought seeing the road was odd, seeing a little city tucked away between the trees is an even odder feeling. There are people here that don't know anything about werewolves or monsters. They've been untouched by the paranormal side of the world. They know nothing about the darkness hiding in the very woods around them. We pause on the fringes looking in and the urge to race forward to look for someone to help me is stronger than it's ever been. I could get away. I glance at James but our faces don't betray that yearning underneath even though I know he must feel it too.

"The rest of you stay here," Dasc says. "I'll phone my contact."

"I could ask around," Brad offers. "Maybe Kelsey passed through here."

A muscle in Dasc's jaw twitches. "Stay here with the others." The tone of his voice makes it clear there is no room for debate. That's too bad. If it had only been Susan left behind to guard James and me, we would've had a chance to escape. We'll have to continue to be patient and wait for a better opportunity to come to us.

Dasc walks forward causally to a nearby gas station and disappears inside. The rest of us wait within the shadows of the trees beyond the reach of the lights from the nearby buildings. Apart from the gas station there's what I think is a bar and what might be a post office. I stare at the small postal service building for a long time. I wonder if I could be clever enough to sneak inside and send a letter to my father. But what possible excuse could I give that the others would believe?

Owls hoot in the distance and small critters rustle the grass as we wait five minutes, then ten, before Dasc appears again. He totes a plastic bag in either hand and passes them over when he reaches us. We split the sandwiches, candy, and drinks amongst ourselves but wait to eat or drink until Dasc finishes off a granola bar first. He nods to give us permission and for once eats alongside us.

He talks around gummies he pops into his mouth. "I made contact with the watch guard at the border. A truck driver crossed into the States with a kid matching Kelsey's description and he's been handed over to the authorities. The watch guard is sending a vehicle our way." He crumples up the empty candy wrapper and stuffs it into one of the plastic bags. "Well, this ought to be interesting getting him back into safe hands."

"But—" I say then bite my tongue. Too late. Dasc's attention is focused squarely on me now. "They won't harm him. He's just a kid."

I expect him to reprimand me like he did Brad earlier. Instead, he sighs and rubs his hands together.

"The world's a complicated and dangerous place, far more than you realize," he says. "The police won't hurt him, but the second the IMS catches wind of his existence, they'll scoop him up, force the serum on him, and stick him in a dark hole because of what he is—that is, if they don't kill him outright. We have to get to him before the IMS does. We protect our own. The pack survives."

"The pack survives," we echo back quietly.

It's not right. If my father found Kelsey, he wouldn't harm him. In fact, what if my father is one of the IMS agents sent to pick up Kelsey?

No. Stop. It's a far off possibility and not likely. I'll keep that potential outcome tucked safely away where I can't get my hopes up too much.

"Rest up," Dasc says. "Our ride won't be here for at least an hour."

We finish off the food he brought and then spread out beneath the trees. I sit propped up against the trunk of a maple with James beside me so close his shoulder touches mine. Neither of us says anything but I can feel the tension in his arm against mine. We have to be ever so careful but this could finally be it. I'm so wound up about it that I can't fall asleep even when I rest there with my eyes closed. The prospects ahead of me are too close and the challenge so intense that my brain can't shut down. I go through possible scenarios in my head and make whatever plans I can. I think of all the things James and I have going for us in the event of an escape but come up with equally negative downsides. We've both been trained to fight and survive in the wild—to hunt, find shelter, know our way—but those are skills Dasc and his followers taught us. Meaning they know the same things and could very well anticipate anything we might do. The best thing we could do would be to do the unexpected.

My thoughts are finally interrupted by the appearance of an SUV rumbling to the very edge of the gas station parking lot closest to where we're hidden. Dasc makes a melodic bird call and one answers from the open window of the vehicle. Together we slip out of the woods and to our waiting ride. Dasc takes the front seat and the rest of us quickly pile in behind him. James and I are shuffled into the back but we both lean forward in our seats to see who our driver is.

A boy probably not much older than ourselves turns about to see who he's shuttling. There's something surly about his face and an odd tinge to his scent. He's a werewolf but he's also . . . something else.

"This everyone?" he asks.

Dasc nods. "I didn't think you'd be the one coming to pick us up."

"I was nearby. Just finished my mission so I was in the area."

Mission? I wonder what sort of mission. And where did he come from?

"This is Rory," Dasc announces for our benefit. "Whisper of the watch guard at the border."

When Dasc mentioned the watch guard earlier, I thought he had friends of some sort watching the border for him. I didn't consider that this group could be made up of other werewolves. If there's a Whisper, then I can only assume there's a whole other compound like the one I came from. Could there really be two places filled with kidnapped children raised to be Dasc's warriors? And if there are two, could there be even more? Why have we never heard of any others?

"So who do we have and where to, boss?" Rory asks.

"This is Susan and Brad." Dasc gestures over his shoulder to them. "And James and Genna are here to help us convince our young Mister Kelsey to return home."

Home. That's where Kelsey is most likely trying to go now. Home isn't in a forest in Canada. It's wherever his true family is. Wisconsin, I think he once mentioned. Minnesota's right next door. So close to my home. So close.

"We'll make for the closest inspection point," Dasc says. "Hopefully the Jackal will get lucky and be able to locate Kelsey for us before we get there."

"International Falls it is," Rory says. "It's going to be a long ride."

Everyone in the vehicle falls silent as we settle in for the journey ahead. I'm left to evaluate every aspect of my current situation, ponder over who the Jackal is, how I might be able to escape with James and Kelsey, and then bring the IMS to the compound in the north. How I might accomplish all of this, I have no idea. I lean back in my seat and try to sleep but it proves difficult. James slips his hand into mine and I thread my fingers through his. Whatever happens, we're in this together. I can count on him. Despite his early failings during combat training, I took it upon myself to help him. He's gotten strong and fast. If it comes to a fight, he can certainly hold his own and will have my back.

The drive is annoyingly long and it's morning by the time we reach the border. We've stopped only once to relieve ourselves and get more gas. We have to hurry. While we wait outside the vehicle with the inspection building in sight, Rory strides away to find one of his contacts. I stretch and close my eyes facing the sun, enjoying its warmth on my skin.

"Dasc," Susan says quietly. "If he is being held by the IMS, what will we do?"

"Whatever it takes but I'd rather not engage a fight. That brings far too much attention. We need to do this quickly and quietly."

"Of course."

It's not long before Rory returns and looks sour. That can't be good.

"The Jackal got in," he announces. "And found out Kelsey managed to escape into Minnesota before the IMS could show up. He's trying to track him down but Kelsey's given him the slip. The boy has maybe three hours head start on us."

"That's both fortunate and unfortunate," Dasc says and sighs. "Out of the reach of the IMS and straight on to other dangers. We need to get to La Crosse as fast as possible."

Rory's eyes grow wide. "La Crosse?"

"That's where Kelsey originally came from. If he's going anywhere, it'll be there."

"But . . . that's where—"

"I know very well what's there, Rory."

He inclines his head. "I'll help you cross the border. I've already made sure a vehicle's waiting on the other side."

"Good."

We pile back into the vehicle and move parallel away from the inspection building. I pay attention closely to exactly how we're getting past the border. The sun's in the sky and there are officials all over the place. Rory takes us away from that and we keep on going until we've gone at least half an hour or more before we finally come to a stop on the edge of a forest. The vehicle is left behind and we head out on foot with our packs. Once we're in the shelter of the trees, Dasc transforms and we follow his lead. Then we run.

I hear a click nearby and my head swivels towards a camera attached to a tree trunk watching the woods. It's then that I understand. The people watching the border are looking for people, not wolves. This way we can pass undetected to the other side through the wilderness. We keep on running for quite some time until at last we reach a car covered in leaves parked at the end of a gravel road. We don't immediately shift back as Dasc and Rory check the surrounding area. Once it's clear, Dasc transforms and everyone follows suit except for Rory.

Dasc lays a hand on his head. "You did well. Head back to the watch guard and keep me informed if you hear anything else."

Rory the wolf bows low and then takes off the way we had come.

"Everyone in," Dasc orders and we pile into the waiting vehicle. "It's going to be another long ride and at the end of it . . . well, we can only hope for the best."

"What's in La Crosse?" I ask.

Dasc merely says, "Vampires, my dear. And Kelsey may be walking right into them."

Vampires. I've learned about them, trained to fight them, but this will be the first time I may actually encounter them. A thrill of excitement and dread goes through me. I worry for Kelsey but I've been needing to satisfy the building bloodlust in my veins for a very long time. Now could be my chance.

The car rumbles along and I try to catch some sleep. I rest my head on James's shoulder for a while and when I wake up, he does the same in turn. We grab food, stop for bathroom breaks, but otherwise make for La Crosse with all speed. It takes me some time to figure out where exactly we are. When I realize we're in Minnesota, the urge to slaughter everyone in the vehicle apart from James and make a run for it becomes almost overwhelming. I'm in Minnesota. Home is here somewhere and with the tag tucked in my shoe, I have a location that I can find. Dad's out there. He's waiting for me, I know it.

But I have no weapon. I don't have a good line of attack on the three others. I consider simply opening the door and flinging myself out, but that wouldn't work either. If Dasc and the others aren't trapped or otherwise unable to follow me, they'd catch me and then the game would be up. They'd never let me have any sort of freedom to try the same thing again.

Patience. I've been good at it so far—so much more than Kelsey—and it's served me well. It's let me receive combat training which I'll need to ensure my escape, it's gained me more freedom at the compound, and it's brought me this far. A little more patience just might get me home.

So I wait like a good soldier in the back of the car as the day goes on. I watch the world outside pass by with hungry eyes. We cut through cities big and small, pass towering buildings, drive alongside a massive lake, and navigate through fields and forests.

At one rest station, I almost get an opportunity to make a run for it with James. Dasc heads inside to make another phone call, Susan fills up the car, and Brad sticks with us as we head for the bathrooms. We could take him on. Brad's a capable werewolf but he's not the best. James and I have a chance of knocking him out—especially as he takes the lead so his back is to us. One well aimed blow is all it would take. I look to James and he nods. He knows this is our best chance too. We'll have a few minutes head start on Dasc and Susan and I saw a police station on our way here. We could make it.

I curl my hand into a fist and walk a little faster to come up directly behind Brad. A punch to his kidney, a hold around his neck to make him pass out, and then dragging his body into the trees behind the gas station. I take a deep breath and pull back my arm.

"We have to move!" Dasc shouts behind us.

Brad whips about and I stumble backwards away from him. I turn about to Dasc and hope my startled reaction comes across as concern at his words and not almost getting caught in attempting to flee. I was so close.

"What's wrong?" Brad asks, completely oblivious to almost being taken out.

"I just got word from a contact in La Crosse," Dasc says as he tugs us back to the car. "The vampires attacked Kelsey.

He's gone into hiding but we have to get there before they get him."

Oh no.

The thought of escaping slips down my list of concerns into second place. We have to save Kelsey. After everything, he doesn't deserve this. He's a lost kid like me and James. He's one of us.

We hurry back to the car and peel out of the parking lot. It's a tense journey the rest of the way. There had been a countdown before but the odds have changed. There's no longer the worry that Kelsey *might* get into danger—he *is* in danger. Every second we waste is one more second that the vampires have to track him down. We gun it through Wisconsin but La Crosse is quite a distance away as Susan tells me and James. We have also—as she explains—crossed into vampire territory. They apparently have lots of nests and gangs in the state.

"What about Minnesota?" James asks, voicing the question I'm thinking but am smart enough not to ask. I'm a curious person and Dasc knows that, but I also can't afford to show too much curiosity about the place I come from in case he suspects that I want to go back. I want to elbow James in the ribs but that would also draw attention to the fact that James asked something he shouldn't have.

Although his question does manage to provoke an odd interaction between the adults in the vehicle. Susan and Brad share an apprehensive look and Dasc has a bland smile on his face as he stares straight ahead while driving.

"There's what I'd like to call an armistice between the werewolves and vampires," Dasc says. "If they don't cross into Minnesota, we won't cross into Wisconsin. There's been a lot of blood between our kind so the armistice was agreed to for everyone's benefit. That's also why it's so dangerous for Kelsey to go to Wisconsin. If they discover a werewolf in what they consider their territory, they'll hunt him down to no end. We're his only chance."

An armistice. I guess it makes sense except for one thing. If the werewolves aren't supposed to go over there, how did Kelsey get turned into a werewolf in the first place if he lived in Wisconsin? Doesn't that mean a werewolf would have gone over there and broken this armistice? Given the look that the adults shared at James's question, I'm sure there's more to this than they're telling us.

"So how do we find him?" I ask.

"Leave that to me," Dasc answers in his usual vague way when asked a direct question. I'm surprised he gave us a straight answer about the armistice actually.

We continue to speed south towards La Crosse. I try to soak in the surroundings outside the car windows, tucking away the information I gather for later in case I ever need it.

It's late by the time we finally reach the sprawling city. My breath fogs the glass as I watch the hundreds of buildings and streets fly past. A real city with real people that are mere feet outside the confines of this trap I've found myself in. The only thing that keeps me from leaping out is the thought of Kelsey being hunted by a ravenous pack of blood suckers. Save Kelsey first, then escape. With other people so close, this is our best chance yet.

The car winds out of the business area and onto quiet

roads lined with houses and neat yards. Dasc pulls into a driveway in front of a blue two-story and parks.

"This is Kelsey's old house," he says quietly. "We'll check here first just in case. Everyone stay alert. There's no telling what we'll find in here."

He exits and we group around him on the walkway to the front porch. He points to the door and I realize it's sitting ajar. There are no lights on inside. I've got a bad feeling about this. Dasc nudges the door open with the toe of his boot and tiptoes inside. Brad goes next, then James and me, and Susan brings up the rear.

My footsteps are near silent on the carpet inside but they stick to something underfoot. I lift one shoe and peer down only to realize there's fresh blood splattered across the floor. I can smell its coppery tang along with the smell of death like a cloud in the cramped air of the house. We walk through the entry and into the living room where we discover the first body. An older man with a plaid shirt, bite marks on his neck and his skin ghostly pale. Dead.

An image of my mother dying in my father's arms flashes through my mind.

My mother's murderer walks carefully around the dead man and into the kitchen where we find a woman face down on the floor, her hand still clutched around a knife coated in black blood. At least she managed to put up a fight before being killed.

"Vampires," James murmurs.

"Vampires," Dasc agrees.

"Why kill them?" I ask.

"Because they were his parents." Dasc gives me a dark look. "You must understand that our enemies will always seek to hurt you in the worst possible way. They go after the ones you care about to make you suffer. By coming here, Kelsey only made them targets."

He continues to walk carefully through the first level of the house inspecting everything and eventually stops at the railing of the stairs where a strip of red cloth is tied to the banister. It must mean something because he trails his fingers over the fabric and looses a sigh.

"They have Kelsey."

"How do you know?" I ask.

He points to the red strip. "Because whenever we have cause to meet at a neutral location, we leave markers like this. Come on. We have to go save our friend."

Our friend, as if Dasc is Kelsey's friend when all Kelsey has ever wanted is to escape him and come home. To this place, where his parents now lie dead.

If I ever make it home, what will I return to? Will my father be targeted because of me?

We hastily exit the house and leave it just as we found it. Dasc takes the wheel once more and we ride south through town into an area made up of looming warehouses. Darkness swallows up most of the buildings but there's one with a light that shines directly over a door on its side. The car comes to a halt outside and Dasc motions for us to exit. Once we do, Susan comes up to my side and puts a hand on my shoulder.

"Perhaps they shouldn't be here for this," she suggests softly.

Dasc shakes his head. "They need to know the truth."

The truth? About what?

But as usual, no one clarifies. Instead, we follow Dasc

into the darkness through the warehouse door. Sawdust covers the floor and the wooden boards creak beneath my footsteps. Metal siding makes up the walls and creates eerie echoes as we walk through a short entryway and into an enormous room.

Only three lights hang from the ceiling high above to illuminate the scene before us. Five vampires stand in a loose group with bloodshot eyes, exposed fangs as they hiss at us, and blood on their lips. One of the males at the back of the group keeps his hands on Kelsey's shoulders who stands shell-shocked, tears streaked through the dirt on his face. He has a nasty bruise blooming on the side of his face and there's dried blood around the collar of his shirt.

One of the vampires steps forward to stand toe to toe with Dasc. "Is red the color of war?"

"It's the color of the blood I'll shed in victory," Dasc responds.

I don't understand what's going on but their strange words must mean something.

"I'm here for the boy," Dasc continues.

The vampires sneer at us.

"And what do we get in return?"

"Your lives."

Their lips pull back to expose their sharp fangs.

Anger boils my blood at the injustice of what's happening. Kelsey's family was slaughtered by these vampires and Dasc wants to make a deal with them. I try to think of what my father would do in this situation. Maybe he would arrest them. Maybe he would kill them if they attacked. But I can hardly consider what my father might do in this position. All I can think of is what *I* want to do to these things before me baring their teeth.

I want to rip them to shreds.

"You got your share of blood," Dasc says and extends a hand towards Kelsey. "Now give us the boy and we'll leave."

My hands curl into fists at the urge to butcher them without remorse. Kelsey got out. He got away and he returned home only to have his family murdered. There's nothing right here. Susan's hand grasps my shoulder to hold me back. It's the only thing reining me in.

The vampires share apprehensive looks and eventually the one holding Kelsey cautiously pushes him towards us. Brad tugs him into the safety of our group. James and I crowd around him to shield him as well. His eyes are dead and stare at nothing in particular. They broke him.

"Thank you," Dasc says with a benign smile. "That wasn't so hard, now was it?"

"Leave this place and take your mutts with you."

"Don't worry. I will." Dasc turns to us as if to usher us out. "Come along." But then he pauses and holds up a finger as if he forgot something. "Oh, but one thing first."

Fast as lightning, he whips out a knife from inside his jacket and hurls it into the chest of the closest vampire. The blood sucker manages to gasp just once before crumpling to the ground. The remaining vampires snarl at the affront. Two immediately rush Dasc while the others go wide eyed and make to run for it.

I can smell their foul blood. A red haze falls over my eyes.

Who I am becomes undone.

I unravel. I transform.

None of those vampires are leaving this room alive.

The next minute is a blur of fur, blood, screams, and the rending of flesh. I don't remember half of what happens, but by the end of it the vampires are dead and I stand on all fours dripping black blood from my mouth. James paces next to me with hackles raised and Dasc in his enormous black wolf form stalks over to us. He's the largest wolf I've ever seen. His eyes gleam with their own golden light.

In an instant he shifts and gets down on one knee to look at me directly. Blood coats his lips.

"This is the truth," he says calmly despite the massacre in the room around us. "There is a war coming, Genevieve, and we are at the heart of it. What happened here is just a taste of what is to come. Our kind will always be hunted. That's why we've trained you and made you strong. To survive, we must be soldiers. We cannot show mercy. We will not apologize. This is only the beginning of the end."

December 22, 2007
Day 4,069

Winter is a cruel and patient beast that feasts upon unprepared souls in the far north. It howls and freezes and destroys. Its icy fingers trap and kill. But there is also beauty and grace wrapped in silence muffled by the thick snow. I sit up on a tree branch coated with ice and watch the dancing shades of the northern lights in the sky. Here, alone in the world, I find a sense of peace and belonging. The world is a wild untamable thing. I like to think we share that in common.

From my icy perch, I can see far and wide over the woods that I know by heart. Everything is layered in thick snow from a storm that recently passed which makes it very easy to spot the tracks I'm searching for. Working on smell alone can be deceiving if one's prey is clever and the wind is right. But fresh snow is hard to beat.

I've been watching a small band of Inuits for the past three days. A group of hunters have ventured too close to the compound for my taste. Normally they keep well away from this area but something has driven them here. While I've been watching them, they've been searching for something or someone. There's a desperate determination to their hunt. When they set up their camp, just before they bed down I see one of them being comforted by the others. I assume the target of their search is due to this man. There's only one explanation that satisfies the puzzle before me. This man is searching for a lost loved one in the frozen wastes.

It's to him that my eyes are so often drawn. Even now, tucked away in the ice shelter he made for himself and at the very edge of my vision on the horizon, I can't help but check to make sure he's all right. Their close proximity to the compound isn't my only concern here.

That's why when I haven't been keeping an eye on them, I've been hunting myself.

My fingers, nose, and toes are stiff from keeping still too long, and the cold has penetrated my many layers. If I were a normal human like those below in the camp, I would have suffered from frostbite long ago. I guess it's a good thing I'm not normal.

I slide down the trunk of the tree and transform just before I hit the ground.

It's time to go hunting.

The band of Inuits has been widening their search each day so it's no surprise the wildlife nearby has become more scarce, but it's not the only reason why. Something else has come into the area that's frightened even the polar bears away. I've found a few skeletons of caribou gnashed to bits by whatever it is. That's why I came out here in the first place. Whatever it is cuts a wide swath of a trail but it always seems to be dragging something to cover up its true markers—the shape of its footprints. At least if I had that, I'd have a better idea of what it is. What I do know is it's big, hungry, and will eat just about anything. I don't want anyone running into it, whatever it is.

I run down tracks for an hour or two before I know I need to get out of the cold and rest for a while. There's no point trying to run all the way back to the compound so I make for an arctic fox's den I discovered some time ago. It's a tight fit but I manage to crawl inside. The fox itself grows agitated when I enter but we've come to a sort of truce— developed a bond even—over the last two winters. I found it after a lynx killed its kits and almost killed it too. I nursed it back to health and have kept the area clear of lynxes since then. I've sometimes found it following me in the Werewood or watching me from afar. It even tolerates me sharing its den on occasion. When I curl up into a ball, the fox maneuvers itself to sleep against my belly, tucked between my front and back paws. I guess more than tolerates my presence.

The night passes in the shelter and relative warmth of the fox's burrow. Before dawn, I rise once more and get breakfast for the two of us as a way of saying thank you. I bring back a pair of rabbits that the fox and I split. My teeth rip into the uncooked meat but it doesn't bother me in the slightest. This is life out here in the wilderness and I am a wolf.

The fox and I part ways as I resume my hunt and keep

an eye on the Inuits doing the same. I come across a wide path cutting through the snow with an odd scent to it. Whatever the thing is, it's getting closer to the compound.

A howl suddenly echoes through the frigid air. My ears pivot to catch the sound and pinpoint exactly where it's coming from. Marking where the trail is, I bound through the thick snow towards the source of the howling. Minutes later I find a lone wolf waiting for my arrival. Almost pure white except for a dusting of silver along the top of his head and down his back, James blends perfectly into his surroundings whereas I stick out like a fly in milk. His tongue lolls out when I approach.

I reach him and paw at his nose. He ducks and makes a panting sound like laughter. As if on cue, we both shift at the same time but remain crouched low in our thick winter jackets. We both have our faces wrapped up in white scarfs and hats pulled down low to fend off the cold when we're not in our thick werewolf coats.

"What are you doing out here?" I ask quietly to match the hush of the woods around us.

James rubs his hands together. "Alex wanted someone to check in with you, see how it was going."

"I don't need my hand held."

"I know. Alex just wants an update on what you've found."

"And he couldn't bother to come out here himself?"

He pulls down his scarf just enough so I can see his smile. "Well, he's a little busy so I volunteered to, you know, take the load off his back."

More like so we could talk privately away from the compound. We don't get the opportunity often but we've had days like this more frequently. Alex has been passing off certain duties to me, like checking out unknown dangers coming too close to the compound. For a while now I've been getting the feeling that Alex is training me in to be a Whisper like him. I've resented it but at the same time I know it's an opportunity to do some good.

Despite the new freedoms afforded to me, I haven't tried to run away. Every time I consider it, I think of Kelsey's family torn apart in their home. Dasc explained to us that we're targeted by other monsters because of what we are. We've been a part of a war all this time without even knowing it. After that dreadful day, we learned the truth about what's out there and waiting for us—and what could happen to the people we love if we put them in danger. Being werewolves puts us at the heart of the conflict, trapped between the forces of the IMS and the monsters under the control of Echidna, the Mother of Monsters. On one side, the IMS fears us so they hunt us. On the other, Echidna wants to wipe out the werewolves because we're a threat to her reign. Our bite is powerful, enough to worry the other monsters out there.

The war is real. I've seen it with my own eyes. Those vampires in La Crosse were just the tip of the iceberg. Other rogue monsters have come looking for trouble, from trolls to really stupid vampires to a shapeshifter. The trolls were killed. The vampires were wiped out almost single-handedly by Kelsey who kills any vampire that comes even remotely close. And turns out the shapeshifter works with Dasc to help safeguard our haven, an ally in the brewing war.

Now there's this huge, lumbering thing in the Werewood somewhere I have yet to unveil.

"I found fresh tracks," I say. "Want to tag along?"

James nods. "Sure." But before shifting, his gaze turns south. "It'd be a good day for it. Running."

I avoid looking south at all. "Yeah."

But I know neither of us will try it. The risk is too great to our families and we have responsibilities here to the other werewolves. They need us. And part me doesn't want to leave this refuge in the snow despite being ashamed of myself for even thinking it. If what Dasc and the others tell us is true, then the rest of the world hates us. The monsters, the normal humans, everyone. The second we try to step foot back into that world, we'll be ostracized or worse. Maybe one day I'll return home to my father, but it's become a fleeting dream in the back of my mind.

Perhaps it wouldn't be so bad staying here after all.

"Come on." I shift before he can say anything else about trying to flee.

He follows suit and I lead him to the trail I had found earlier. Unfortunately, we're not the only ones who have discovered the trail. The Inuits appear through the woods pointing silently to the wide path and begin following it with renewed vigor. I guess that confirms we're both after the same thing. Perhaps one of their kin was attacked by this creature that now threatens my pack and they seek to end it. I've no problem with putting an end to whatever beast we're chasing but their presence adds another complication. They'll either get killed by this thing or will discover us and then . . . well, Dasc might end them to keep our secret safe.

Deciding to keep our distance for the time being and observe, I sink low to the ground and stay well back from the hunters with James at my side. We move along silently in the path of disturbed snow ever watchful. The hunters move slowly and all the while dark storm clouds gather overhead brought in by a growing wind that whistles through the trees. An hour passes, then another, and the wind turns into a powerful force that overturns the tracks. The storm clouds surround us to unburden themselves and worsen the lowering visibility.

James and I are built for this kind of weather but regular humans are not. As we continue to keep our distance—but closer now with the driving snow to hide both us and our prey—I watch the Inuits begin arguing amongst each other. It's clear to me that most want to stop and build a shelter to wait out the storm. However, one man—the man they comfort each night and who drives this hunt—refuses to stop. He's a fool to keep on going. The trail we've been following has nearly vanished and we'll all be buried in the snow before long. There's no point trying to continue and yet he does. When the rest quickly hollow out a drift in which to huddle together, the man slips away into the whiteout. He's going to get himself killed.

I shouldn't go after him. He's chosen his own fate.

And yet . . .

James whines at me when I rise to follow the lone hunter continuing the search. I just whip my tail in his face and head out.

Even with my acute eyesight, it's difficult to track the man when I can hardly see ten feet ahead of me. I'm forced to follow him closely. He struggles ahead with a spear in hand that he uses as a walking stick. His other arm he hoists in front of his face to use as a shield against the wind and snow. He doesn't get far before he's forced to stop. The trail's gone. He drops to his knees with a wail. I watch his despair in the midst of the whirling snow and feel my own frozen heart start to thaw.

I'm so focused on the man that I almost miss the giant shadow behind him. It would have been easy to miss as it so easily blends into the woods with its icy blue skin except for the fact that it moves. The wailing man doesn't notice the monstrosity reaching for him.

I rush through the blinding snow with a resounding bark and rush for the man. He startles and hastily gets to his feet, backing away with his spear held before him. When he finally notices the shadow reaching for him, he shouts something in obvious panic and rushes in the direction of his comrades. The giant thing I still can't quite make out looks between me and the man as if deciding which meal would be more appetizing. But if that giant follows the man, not only will he be killed but the rest of the Inuits with him.

I'm faster than that man and know these woods. I have a better chance of standing up to it.

Rushing forward, I nip at the giant's feet and get a fleeting look at it. It stands at twice the height as the Inuit man with skin the color of cracked ice on a deep lake. Blood stains its fingers and lips, and it's wrapped in a cobbled collection of animal skins. A frost giant. I've never seen one in person before but I know of them through my training.

That's the most I see before I'm forced to run for my life. His hand snatches down faster than I anticipate and almost grabs my tail. I take off like a dart through the snow storm that's both a blessing and a curse. It's hard for me to see but I hope it's also harder for this frost giant to see me. I bark now and then to get it to follow, hoping it won't change its mind and go after the man instead. In the distance, James barks as well. Good. Hopefully that'll confuse it. I run a ways with my tracks being blown over by the snow until I come to an acceptable tree. Shedding my wolf self, I climb and climb and climb until I hear the frost giant coming near. I stop and press up tight to the trunk. It pauses near the foot of the tree, looks this way and that. Then its eyes turn upward. I don't move and hope that with my white gear and the flurry he won't be able to see me. His gaze passes right over where I hide, scans the nearby trees, and then he stomps on.

I don't take his moving on for granted and I don't let my guard down. He could easily be waiting me out. So, instead I wait as well clinging to that tree and wishing I could be back in the fox's den as the wind whips any exposed skin raw. James doesn't bark in the distance anymore or make any sound to tell me where he is. But that also doesn't tell the frost giant where he is either.

When I've waited for as long as I can in the brutal storm, I slip down the tree and search for shelter. Shifting back into my wolf self, I dig a snow cave beneath the branches of a spruce tree and curl up on myself out of the wind. I keep my ears pricked for any sounds of the frost giant returning to find me. He doesn't but the storm continues to rage on and on. The day drags on and my stomach growls. The light eventually fades, night settles in, and the wind continues to howl. The entrance I made is swept over and I'm lost in my own little bubble beneath the spruce needles and snow.

I hope James found somewhere to bed down safely and that the frost giant decided to give up hunting for the day.

My thoughts keep turning to that man so desperate to find this frost giant. I wonder . . . if this thing's been eating random beasts and even went for that man, perhaps it took someone that man cares about. He's refused to stop looking. Who knows how long he's been at it? How much does he care for this person that he's willing to sacrifice everything for?

Has my own father still been searching for me after all this time? Does he have such dedication as that poor man? If so, why has he not found me? Did he stop looking?

I lay my tail over my nose and wish such thoughts didn't occur to me.

I'm not sure how much time passes before the constant howl diminishes. I scratch out a hole in my shelter to be able to test the air outside. The storm has passed and in it's a wake another foot of snow is left behind. After making sure the coast is clear, I check my surroundings. There's no sign of the frost giant or the Inuits. I hope the latter found some safe place out of harm's way.

First things first. Breakfast. Then I need to find James so he can return to the compound with news of the frost giant. I'll need to stay out here and keep an eye on it once I locate it again. After downing a beaver near one of the frozen streams, I try to pick up a scent on James. He wouldn't have gone all the way back already without knowing I'm okay. But the storm's wiped away traces of everything in its path.

I'm in the middle of widening a circle search pattern when I find something unexpected. Not the Inuits, not the frost giant, not James. Strangers. Humans. A teenage boy and a man. We hardly, if ever, get hikers in this area. People are smart enough to know that it's dangerous in these parts, mostly because of us, and yet here they are both bundled up against the cold with big packs on their backs.

A new possible threat or new potential victims of the frost giant.

Both curious and cautious, I keep my distance while keeping an eye on the pair. Hunkered low in the thick snow with my ears perked forward, I follow them as a silent and stealthy shadow. Neither of them picks up on my presence but I've been trained for this. Once I know who they are and where they're going, I'll slip away to find James and the frost giant again. The pair of hikers remain quiet as they struggle through the waist high snow and use poles to assist them.

My keen ears pick up their soft and muffled conversation.

"Damn storm," the man grumbles. "I was so close to finding it."

"It's a giant," the teenager says somewhat crossly. "There can't be too many places for it to hide."

So they're searching for the frost giant same as me. That complicates things.

"When I want your *expert* opinion, I'll ask for it."

"You're the one who wanted me to come along."

"So you'd stop complaining about being stuck in Dreamland. Besides, you need field experience. You need to understand what's really out there."

The teenager shakes his head. "I found that out a long time ago."

They come to a halt as the man gives a big sigh and looks around at the trees. He points with one of the poles in his hand to a towering pine. "Why don't you make yourself useful and get us a bird's eye view?"

One second the boy is there.

The next he vanishes.

Startled, I quickly assess the landscape and realize he's reappeared in the very same pine tree the man had pointed to. He crouches on one of the branches with a hand braced against the trunk to get a good look at the ground below. I shrink down into the snow and don't dare move lest he spot me. As I take shallow breaths, I consider this boy's apparent ability to teleport from one spot to another. There's only one way it could be possible. He's one of the Blessed, the pawns and warriors of the dragons granted the gift of magic.

If he's a Blessed, then I can assume one other thing about him.

He works for the International Monster Slayers.

These two out in the middle of these forlorn woods hunting down a frost giant are agents. This is more complicated than I thought. Scaring off a pair of hikers is one thing. Having agents in our midst is . . . well, it's . . .

I can't keep my eyes off the boy as he vanishes once again and reappears at his companion's side. What little I can see of his face and hear of his voice, he sounds young, far younger than I imagined an IMS agent would be. The man looks much more the type.

I wonder if they know who Agent Jefferson Barnes is.

Could this be the opportunity I've been waiting for?

Surely they have some kind of remote communication with them. If I made contact, they could radio in the IMS and even my father.

And then—

Liberate the entire compound. Protect our families.

My chest aches and everything inside me feels wrong, bent out of shape. I've wanted desperate freedom for so long but when it presents itself this way, I can't help but worry. The last time one of us got close to freedom, everything fell apart at our feet. And each day I've been here, I've been reminded that we need to keep ourselves safe, not only from monsters but the IMS. I've been told I'll be dragged away and injected with a serum to control me or make me suffer. When something's been told to you every day for years on end, even a glimmer of the truth from the distant past can be easily crushed by swaying doubt. What if the others are right? What if the IMS is dangerous? Do I dare take that chance and put the lives of werewolves at the compound in jeopardy?

Deep longing stirs in my chest for a place I once called home where I had a mother and father who loved me. But I am patient. I've had to be for ten years now.

So I remain patient.

I keep an eye on the pair of agents as they trudge through the thick snow and try to pick up the trail of the frost giant. They stop talking and focus on the task at hand. I want them to keep talking though. I want to know more about them, about the IMS, about everything. There are too many variables to consider in each choice I could make. I need as much information as I can if I'm going to make the right decision.

Nearing midday, James finds me instead of the other way around. He crawls up beside me and his eyes immediately lock on to the pair of agents in the near distance. Not bothering to shift to explain the situation, I make some marks in the snow with my paw. Making the symbol for the compound, I point at James then the mark and shoo him away. Another symbol for scouting and a point at the agents, he nods in understanding. He nudges me with his shoulder before sneaking back the way he came. He'll inform the compound of what I'm up to and what we've found. But he doesn't know who these people are that I'm tracking. That detail I'm keeping to myself—even hiding it from James of all people—until I can decide if I can trust them or not.

The two agents rarely talk and from what little they do say, I get the distinct impression that they don't like each other much. Simmering hostility is behind every word they say in clipped sentences, the man always goading the teenager. I watch with fascination as the boy teleports here and there to get a better view of the forest around them. At one point he lingers overlong up on a tree branch gazing forlornly into the distance.

"Charlie," the man grouses. "Come on."

The teenager—Charlie—grumbles something and teleports back to the man's side.

"What did you say?" the man asks sharply.

"Nothing."

The tension rises between the two and I sneak along behind them. My paws ache with the cold so I pause when I can to curl them in one at a time to my chest to warm back up. My stomach grumbles and the pair eventually stops to break for lunch. They roll out a tarp to sit on in the shelter of a snow drift and unwrap sandwiches. They munch quietly within reluctant proximity to each other. The breakfast I had this morning seems so long ago now and saliva gathers in my mouth.

"Laurence—"

"Uncle Laurence," the man says sharply. "Show a little respect."

So that's it. Nephew and uncle. I wonder what happened to have formed such animosity between them. Charlie the teenager looks like he wants to stab his walking pole through his uncle's face.

"What happens after this?" Charlie asks.

His uncle takes his time chewing before responding. "After what?"

"After we kill the frost giant."

"Then hopefully the IMS finally grants my request and I go hunting. I could take you with, show you how it's done."

Charlie looks a little green at the thought of hunting whatever it is his uncle has suggested, and he sets his sandwich on his leg as if he's lost his appetite. Laurence keeps chomping away at his sandwich until it's gone.

"Don't look so sour," he says and smacks his lips. "You ought to jump at the chance to hunt werewolves."

My heart skips a beat.

"Why should I?" the nephew says bitterly.

"You know very well why," Laurence snaps. He dusts off his hands and levels his full attention on his nephew. "The serum? Being taken off the monster kill list? It's all nonsense and we both know that. Once it's in their blood, they're rotten inside. It's a mercy to everyone to just put them out of their misery. Even your—"

"*Stop.*"

His uncle smiles. "What, you some kind of werewolf enthusiast now?"

"I don't want anything to do with werewolves." Charlie grabs his sandwich, rises, and marches away.

"So that's why?" his uncle calls after him. "Afraid they'll remind you of someone?"

The nephew doesn't respond.

I hunker down even lower as any hope I might have had in the two withers into ashes. Even if I made contact and explained about the kidnapped children, they wouldn't help. No, one would want to hunt us down and the other wouldn't lift a finger. We're just beasts to them. Maybe the other werewolves are right about the IMS.

I remain hidden as the two eventually pack up their tarp and continue on their hunt for the frost giant. The others should know of the danger these agents pose. Turning tail, I sneak back through the woods in the direction of the compound. The wind shifts directions and a scent catches my attention. There's no mistaking who it is.

Dasc.

I wait patiently for him to show himself. He must have gotten back while I've been out in the woods. I suspect he's looking for me if James managed to pass along word of what we discovered. Silent as a shadow, he slips between the trees directly to me. In his wolf form he's almost double my size. A giant among werewolves.

A giant I intend to one day fell.

We both shift when he reaches me.

"James told me what you found out here," he says immediately. "Any sign of that frost giant? Or those hikers?"

"I lost sight of the frost giant," I say and exhale sharply. My breath rises as a fine mist. "But those hikers are IMS agents. They're after the frost giant too."

His eyes flash yellow and his attention turns razor sharp to the woods around us. "Where are they?"

Without him even saying anything I can see where this is going. "If we kill them, their absence will be noted. Others could come looking for them. If they finish their hunt, they'll go away."

"Perhaps you're right, but I fear their hunt will still lead them to us."

"Maybe if we . . . if we managed to drive the frost giant elsewhere, they'd follow."

I hope Dasc decides to be the one to volunteer for that job. Let the two of them fight and kill one another. To my surprise, he actually does.

"I'll find it and *persuade* it to leave," he says. "Keep an eye on those agents. If they get too close to the compound, I want you to take care of them."

I nod without hesitation. Hesitating would mean that I don't agree with his orders or might refuse to do them. He looks me over just once before shifting and taking off at a swift lope between the trees. I'll keep an eye on the agents, sure, but I'm not going to kill them if it comes to that. There are always other ways to deal with intruders.

It's not difficult picking up the trail again and finding the pair still on the hunt. They stop frequently to eat snacks and warm up. Lying low in the snow once again, I keep my eyes on them lest they turn towards the hidden compound and discover something they're not supposed to. My stomach growls and I tuck in on myself to fight off the creeping chill that's always lingering up here. Paws aching, I get up to move now and then to keep my blood flowing. It's after one such walk that I return to find the agents have discovered something.

"Keep your lighter handy," the man says to his nephew. "We set this thing on fire or we don't make it out of these woods alive."

"I got it," the nephew snaps.

They've discovered fresh tracks of the frost giant—tracks that will undoubtedly lead them right to the frost giant while Dasc is talking to it. Then the giant will be the least of their worries. Dasc will kill them on the spot. For everyone's sake, I quickly sneak away and once I'm out of sight, I race on ahead in a wide loop until I find the trail again further on ahead of the pair. I'll need to get there first, make sure the frost giant is on the move, and that Dasc is nowhere to be seen. I make sure to drag my feet and muddy my tracks amidst that of the giant's wake. The less those agents know the better.

I head deep into the woods, further than I ever have before in this direction. Soon I'm amongst unfamiliar trees and strange landmarks. The light turns gray and heavy clouds roll in once again. I'm starting to wonder if I'll actually come across the frost giant before Dasc when I hear a booming voice up ahead. I can't quite make out the words but the voice sounds angry.

Traveling at a low crouch to hide in the thick snow, I come to a cave entrance curtained by jagged icicles, some of which have broken off as if a large creature—like a giant—hit them with its head when going in. I slink to the side of the entrance and peer into the dark. My eyes adjust to find bones littered before me, lining the cave and amassing in a great pile near the back. Before it stands the giant I came across earlier and across from him is Dasc looking rather irritated.

"You're being entirely irrational," Dasc says and plants his hands on his waist.

"This is mine," the giant thunders and points to the ground beneath him. "You'll not scare me, tiny wolf."

Dasc's snarl echoes in the cave. "Do you not know who I am?"

"I know." The giant turns away from him and picks up a nearby bone—a femur—to start gnawing on.

"Then doing as I ask is working in your best interests."

The giant snorts and the bone cracks between his teeth. "I don't do your dirty work like the vampires."

My head empties and the giant's words tumble over and over in the darkness left behind.

"Head west," Dasc says calmly. "There's a small town without any IMS protection."

"Children?"

"Several."

The giant harrumphs and picks at his teeth with the broken bone as he thinks it over.

"You must go at once," Dasc continues. "Unless you want a couple of agents to set you on fire. They're closing in on you as we speak."

The giant slams a fist on the ground. "I'll crush them!"

"You will leave," Dasc says darkly. "Or I'll make sure you die a long, slow, painful death. Then I'll head to your homeland and do the same to the rest of your kin. Every. Single. One."

The wind whispers through the trees for a long moment before the giant rises, his head brushing the roof of the cave, and says, "Fine, tiny wolf. I'll go."

"Right now."

With one last harrumph, the giant stomps to the entrance. I slink back to hide as it strides through the snow with the broken bone still in its massive hand. Once it's thirty yards off, Dasc emerges from the cave. I shift and walk up to his side but he doesn't startle.

"I thought I told you to keep an eye on the agents," he says with a lethal calm.

"I was," I say. "But then they picked up the trail and were heading here. I came to make sure you got out before they arrived. Look."

Sure enough, in the distance the giant yells as two dark shapes run after him. A flaming arrow blazes through the gray light and the sounds of their fight die away into the far woods.

"Well, that's one nuisance taken care of," Dasc says with a sigh, hands in his pockets. "We'll let them have their fun. Come on."

"Actually, I . . ." He pauses and his eyes flash yellow in my direction. "I was going to stay and keep an eye on that group of Inuits, make sure they leave too."

Dasc throws an arm around my shoulders and gives me a squeeze. "Keeping an eye out for the others?"

"Always."

He smiles and it makes my gut twist unpleasantly. "That's my girl."

With a final wink, he shifts and bolts through the woods towards the compound.

My legs shake and I walk stiffly into the giant's cave out of the wind. The carefully constructed lies tangled about my life begin to unwind and reveal the truth underneath. The frost giant said the vampires do Dasc's dirty work. Dasc didn't deny it. My eyes burn as I realize what I've done— that I stopped fighting so hard because of what happened to Kelsey's parents. The war between us and the rest of the world became too clear.

But it was a lie.

There is no war between vampires and werewolves. As with everything else, they're in his pocket. And if they do as he asks, then he had them kill Kelsey's parents. All because Kelsey ran away. Dasc, so controlling as he is, just couldn't stand that, could he? So he stripped Kelsey of the one thing he wanted most and fed him the lie that the vampires are the real enemy.

I've lost sight of who I need to fight. I had promised myself and James a long time ago that we would make it home. And I promised myself that I would end Dasc. Now it's become crystal clear that in order to make it home, we have to kill Dasc. We can't leave any other way because he'll hunt us down, he'll make us pay for betraying him.

I think of that Inuit man looking for someone he loves lost in the wilderness. No matter the odds, no matter the dangers, he keeps looking. It makes me ashamed of myself.

Tears sting my eyes. I pick up a nearby bone and hurl it at the wall. Falling to my knees amidst the remains of so many, I grasp at my hair and curl down to my knees.

This will not be my life. My life does not belong to Dasc. My will is my own.

And my will shall never be broken.

I leave the cave with my insides on fire and hands curled into fists. True to my word, I walk through the woods until I find the group of Inuits again. Waiting in the darkness in my black wolf form, I watch from a distance as the group falls asleep with one on guard. The night stretches on but still I wait until the man seeking his loved one is the guard.

Through the darkness, I walk forward until I'm twenty feet away. I stand there until the man's eyes spot me. He stiffens and grasps the spear lying beside him. He doesn't immediately wake the others. I hope he recognizes me, perhaps understands that I saved him from the frost giant before. I gesture with one paw in an awkward motion for him to come. He stands but doesn't move. I gesture again and take a few steps back. When he still doesn't follow, I lie down and roll onto my back to show I don't mean him harm. I get up once more, gesture with my paw, and take a few steps back.

He looks to his companions, but then follows with a torch in one hand.

We keep a respectful distance away from each other but the man continues after me. Together we walk silently beneath the trees for what feels like hours. I follow my own trails until we end up exactly where we need to be. The giant's cave looms before us, its mouth an open void of darkness. The man pauses—rightfully so—but I try to urge him onward. He's followed me this far.

Holding his dying torch aloft, he steps carefully into the cave. He gasps as he beholds the bones, then a cry rips out of him. He stumbles forward in the darkness, falls to his knees, and picks up a shredded fur jacket.

"*Amka!*" he cries. Clutching the jacket to his chest, he rocks back and forth. "*Amka, Amka, Amka…*"

I stand in the entrance as a black shadow watching his grief unfold. No more will he walk these desolate woods clinging to fragile hope. There was never going to be a happily ever after ending to this tale, so I offered him the only thing I could—closure. His search is at an end.

Mine is only just beginning. I don't know where the end of my path will lead. It could very well end with my death. But one thing is certain. I've been reminded of where home truly lies and I will fight for it no matter what stands in my way.

And the way home is through Dasc's dead body.

May 5, 2009
Day 4,569

Susan once told me that you can lead a horse to water but you can't make it drink. Well, I've come up with a saying of my own. You can lead a person to the truth but you can't make them accept it. James and I have been discovering that the hard way lately. When someone has been fed a lie often enough, they can't even remember what the truth looks like anymore. The others in the compound—those like Rosalyn and Kelsey—have let go of what their home used to be as if it's some hazy dream they don't wish to linger on. They act as if the only home they've ever known is here with the werewolves.

Even after a year of trying to convince Kelsey of the truth, he refuses to acknowledge that Dasc had his parents killed. He went through a physical growth spurt and is a force to be reckoned with but he's also erased the little boy that tried to escape to his home and family. He's forgotten who he is and where he came from.

He's not the only one. Rosalyn acts as if she never had a brother who doted on her. No, she's replaced her brother with Alex and is always trying to win his attention. She's been losing that battle to me, though, much to her chagrin.

Rosalyn and I stand elbow to elbow as we wash the dishes from breakfast. She scrubs harder, makes more of a soapy mess, and tries to finish before I do. I let her. I don't really care. What I do care about is Kelsey and James on the other side of the basin drying the dishes. Kelsey keeps his head down but James's eyes flick to me every now and then. We're both waiting for the right opportunity to talk to Kelsey and make another plea to him. What's been made obvious to both of us is that even if we manage to kill Dasc somehow, the wolves will never be free of his influence unless they take that step themselves. The battle for their freedom feels like a fight we're bound to lose, but I won't ever stop fighting.

Whenever I have my doubts, I remind myself of my mother and Kelsey's parents.

"Done!" Rosalyn announces triumphantly. She gives my remaining dishes a haughty look then strides away rather proud of herself. I shake my head.

Kelsey glances up once he realizes that he's alone with James and me, then begins to dry the dishes at a manic pace. I think he realizes what's coming next and he'd rather not be cornered by us again. I've been trying to think of better ways to open his eyes but without proof I can physically show him, it's difficult to even get him in the same room anymore. He doesn't want to think about his parents again, about the pain still underneath, and therefore chooses to remain blind.

"How's the leg?" James asks to open up the conversation while he slowly dries off a plate.

Kelsey shrugs and doesn't make eye contact. "Better."

"That's good."

"Better than those vampires for sure," I add. Kelsey got his leg sliced when off hunting vampires some fifty miles away. Alex told him not to go and went to haul him back. Kelsey's been stuck on kitchen duty for the last two weeks because of it. "Do you ever wonder—"

"I don't want to talk," Kelsey says abruptly and slams down the last bowl.

James sets his rag aside as my hands still in the water of the basin. Before either of us can make any sort of attempt to get through to him, Alex of all people walks in. The three of us straighten and Alex nods his acknowledgment in our direction. He gestures silently with one finger to me. Drying off my hands on a nearby towel, I follow him out of the kitchen with one last look over my shoulder at the boys. James shrugs.

"Let's go for a walk," Alex says simply.

That's all he ever says and I know that it's time for another lesson. Ever since the incident with the frost giant, Alex has been giving me private lessons and tutorials focused on molding me into another one of Dasc's Whispers. I've resented it, hated it to know that I've been chosen to be one of Dasc's prized tools, but it also has given me a position of power within the compound. And with that power comes a leeway of freedom and knowledge which I plan to use for my own purposes at the proper time.

We walk step in step out through the eastern tunnel, pass the guards, and transform to run out to the trees. I do relish this part of running relatively free. Our legs stretch out to their fullest and we race each other beneath the gnarled branches and through tangled brush. The snow has become a mucky mush as spring comes upon the land and grass peeks up hopefully. The crisp winter air is transforming with the smells that come when the warmth comes—wet dirt, decaying leaves, and all the things long since buried that reappear from beneath the melting snow.

I keep my eyes open, always aware of my surroundings and what's out here. The woods have been too quiet for my taste the last week or so. If I've learned anything, it's that danger is everywhere.

Eventually we reach a rocky pool fed by a short waterfall. Alex shifts into his human self and I follow his lead to walk onto the stretch of flat stone beside the water. Like every other time we've come here, Alex immediately attacks. I was caught off guard the first time but I'm prepared for it now. It's become a dance. We spar and train harder than any of the others in the compound. If we are to lead, then we are to lead from the front lines—or so I've been told. Faith can readily be lost in a leader that sits on the sidelines and gives commands. We are to be out in the action whenever this war that's brewing reaches us. Although I've seen my share of monsters, I've never had a sense that there's a war going on despite Dasc insisting on it for the last ten or so years. I'll take pleasure in using these hard earned skills against him some day.

"That's enough for now," Alex finally pants.

We split apart both breathing hard. Alex closes his eyes

and turns his face towards the sun as I stretch out my arms and legs.

"You've been doing well," he comments.

"Thank you."

"Rosalyn keeps insisting she could best you."

I snort. "I'm sure she does."

A faint smile touches his lips. "It's time for another history lesson."

He takes a seat cross-legged on the stone and I mimic his posture opposite him. Once we're both settled, he clears his throat.

"Remind me what we last talked about," he says.

"The ancient hunter families in Europe and the noble dragon hierarchy."

"Excellent memory." He gives me a rare smile and we begin.

It's been like this for a while now. We sit here for hours on end. He talks. I listen. It's to prepare me, he says, so I'm ready to take up the burden of leadership when the time comes—though I don't know when that'll be. Alex isn't old by any stretch of the imagination or in need of a replacement. He's aged but he's aged well. I remember when I first saw him and had to wait for him to eat before I could. I hated him. I hated everything about this place. Over time I've realized just how much he cares for the werewolves under his charge. He truly believes in being their—*our*—protector. For that I've come to respect him. I can almost forgive him for being Dasc's pawn, willing to take on a role of leadership and carry out the devil's orders when he's away.

But isn't that what I'm doing? Isn't that what we're all

doing? Playing this game to stay safe? I've created my own illusions about myself to fool the others. Perhaps I'm not the only one. Sometimes I like to think that I'm not the only one in this fight apart from James, but it's a hope I don't let myself give into. Giving into that line of thought and believing there are others like me is a dangerous gambit, one which could cost me everything if I ever decided to place my trust in the wrong people.

So I listen. I learn about the noble dragons and their ever so proud lineage. I learn about the power plays they continue to make on Draco and the other majestic dragons still active in the world. I wonder at the fate of Terra and Eris, two majestics that disappeared after betraying Dasc in the final battle against Echidna. I hear of other werewolf compounds and how to approach them if ever need be, but I'm not told where they are. It's for our safety, I'm told, to ensure that the strength of the pack lives on in case one should fall or be betrayed from within. I guess that makes sense. Dasc *ought* to be paranoid about people like me seeking to bring his empire down. This one little practice is certainly working against my plans. How am I supposed to save them all if I don't even know where they are?

After hours of stories, we spar some more before hunting for our lunch. Once we've killed, gutted, and feasted on a deer, we return to stories of ancient monsters that Alex warns may rise once again when the war begins.

"How will we know?" I ask. "When the war starts? How will we know it's coming?"

I've never interrupted before. Alex blinks in surprise and angles his head as if thoroughly considering my question.

"When the lamia appear," he says after a moment of contemplation. "They're the harbingers of Echidna's eminent return. Always beware the thirteen, Genna. Where one falls, another takes its place. There will *always* be thirteen."

I know. I've been told many times before. They're almost like ghost stories Dasc will tell us of the women who drink magical blood and steal the powers of others.

"But we don't know when they'll appear," I say.

"No one does. And that's why . . ." Alex angles his head to stare at the pool beside us. Shadows fall across his face and he looks forlorn. "That's why we must always be prepared. And always have the soldiers we need."

Meaning . . . werewolves. Meaning . . . more children taken like me to be raised as Dasc's pawns.

"It's about time again," Alex says softly. "In a few years the next Gathering will happen."

Gathering. That's what they call it?

About that time again . . .

That's when it hits me.

What happened to me, James, Rosalyn, Kelsey, and the other kids wasn't a one-time thing. Of course it wasn't. If Dasc always needs fresh soldiers, then this "Gathering" of children to turn into soldiers must be some kind of cycle so he always has young blood to fight this war. I picture it and the images scroll before my eyes as I close them. Alex, Susan, and their lot must have been the wave before us, taken as children and raised by the wave before them. An endless cycle in anticipation of a war that no one knows when it'll come. How long has this been going on? Decades? Centuries? Since the last great war with Echidna?

How many children like me have been ripped from

their homes? How many families torn apart? How many children raised to live and die as weapons?

A wheel that turns and turns and crushes everything in its path as it spins.

"You understand now," Alex says.

I open my eyes and find him studying me. When I don't say anything, he continues in a soft voice I've rarely heard him use.

"Every cycle Dasc goes to gather freshly turned werewolves and guide them to sanctuaries like this. He offers them freedom from the oppression of the IMS and trains them to defend themselves and the rest of the world. This is our fight, even if we didn't know it when we were young."

Except for one thing. Dasc is the one spreading the werewolf disease. He's not offering them freedom. He's changing them to suit his needs. Does Alex not realize this? Do none of the others?

"How did it happen for you?" I ask. A careful question.

"I was outside playing with my little brother. Our parents weren't home yet and it was getting late, but we stayed outside trying to fish in a stream behind our house." He pauses and his eyes turn to the water again. I'm surprised he's actually telling me the details of his experience. Every other werewolf shrugs off the experience as if they don't care or remember how they were bitten. A werewolf bit them and they wound up here. The end.

Alex's eyes harden and his fingers clench the fabric of his pants.

"A pair of wolves came out of nowhere and attacked us. We were both bitten then left there to shift."

"And the wolves?"

"Disappeared into the trees. Ran right to a third wolf I almost missed except I saw its eyes in the darkness. Two beacons of yellow staring at me."

From the way he says it . . . he knows. He knows exactly who was behind the attack on him and his brother. If he does, then why play Whisper to Dasc? Why not do something about it?

"Two days later, I ran," Alex continues. "So did my brother but we became separated somehow. That was the last time I saw him."

When Alex finally lifts his eyes again, I see myself reflected in them. The man I thought most loyal to Dasc has really been playing the same game I have. I see in him the painful truth he's managed to keep hidden for so long. He's done what he has in order to find his brother.

"You've looked for him." Another careful statement without giving myself away.

He nods. "I have."

"And?"

"I wouldn't be surprised if he's at another compound somewhere, but you know how this works. We don't know about the other compounds and they don't know about us. To keep us safe. To keep the fight going."

"Even as Whisper, you don't know?"

"Even as Whisper," he says quietly.

My heart plummets into the soles of my feet. All my careful planning suddenly feels so wasted. The only reason I've stopped running was to find the rest and free them. But if this . . . if I can't . . .

My eyes turn south.

"But perhaps," Alex says so softly I almost don't hear. "Perhaps someone more clever than me could find them. If only they had the courage and the means to try. If only they realized how someone chose them above all others, and how they might be the one to unite the wolves."

Blood thunders in my ears. Is he saying what I think he is? He nods just once as if he knows exactly what I'm questioning in my mind. He thinks I could do it. He also thinks Dasc chose me above all others. Why? Why me? What makes me special in his devil yellow eyes?

"What's your brother's name?" I ask.

"Dustin, but you'll know him by Rusty Dusty."

"I'd like to meet him someday."

"As would I."

He looks like he wants to say more but he stiffens at the same time the breeze carries a scent to my nose.

Smoke.

We both launch to our feet and scan the darkening skies. There. A rising plume of black smoke to the north.

"The compound," Alex breathes.

In an instant we both shift and start running as fast as our legs can carry us. With each step, the smell of smoke becomes stronger and the light wanes. How long has a fire been burning? What's happened? Are the others safe? We run and run until the glowing flickers of flame are in sight. Alex slows and I move at a fast crouch beside him. When we reach the edge of the wood cover, we pause to take in the sight before us.

Smoke billows out from two of the hidden exits of the compound, flames crawl forth from spots where the tunnels have collapsed, and the air is thick with an acrid smell that burns my sensitive nose. My ears pick up the sounds of fighting, snarling, howls, and sharp cries of pain from within.

I let my werewolf instincts override everything else within me. I'm ready to tear our enemies apart and leave nothing but a trail of blood in my wake.

Alex nips at my foreleg and then sprints for the eastern entrance. I chase after him and we remain low to the ground. At the entrance we find the first of the invaders standing watch. They're humanoid on first glance but then I see the long claws on the tips of their fingers, the feathers that line their arms and faces, the oddly luminous eyes that sweep the area. Harpies. Three of our watchers lay dead at their feet in messy piles of blood.

Before they can spot us, we leap from the shadows and sink our teeth into their backs. They squawk for only a moment before we have them on the ground and their throats ripped out. As soon as the first threat is cleared, we slink further into the compound in search of the others and any intruders foolish enough to have come here. We're forced to take certain pathways since some of the tunnels have collapsed or fires rage within. As we go, we come across more bodies scattered across the floor—some harpies, some wolves. Each wolf I recognize and it only adds to the ferocity boiling my blood.

They've killed members of my pack. There's no force on earth that will stop me from tearing them apart.

The bloodlust drives me on past the wretched smells and burning smoke filling my nostrils. Sounds of battle draw us in deeper. We come across several harpies wandering in pairs and slicing at the bodies of the fallen with their long claws. Alex and I make sure they don't remain breathing for long. My body moves on instinct from so many long hours of training. I just never thought I'd be fighting the battle in the middle of the compound.

Before long we come across a few survivors that have managed to hold their own. Cornered in the kitchen, we find Kelsey, James, and two others surrounded by corpses of harpies. We bark to each other then all shift.

"We thought you were dead," Kelsey pants.

"Where are the others?" Alex asks.

"Last we knew, they were heading for the armory," James says. "You have to be careful. I think they have wolfsbane on their claws. Anyone who's been scratched goes down."

Alex and I exchange a glance. We've been lucky so far but we need to adapt our strategy.

"Make for the Werewood," Alex commands in a rough voice. "Pick up any other survivors you can and lay low."

Kelsey bares his teeth. "I'm not running from a fight."

The look Alex gives him could have melted steel. "We've already lost this fight. Now we save whoever we can. We've cleared the way. Go."

"We should go with you," James says and glances at me. "Help rescue the others."

"Just get to the Werewood. *Now.*"

Clearly reluctant to pull out of the fight, James and the others shift into wolves once more to hurry out of the kitchen to the eastern exit.

Alex lays a hand on my shoulder as he watches them go. "Let's get to the armory."

We shift together and head further into the compound.

Each roadblock we hit turns us in another direction but I realize it all seems to be leading us to the armory as if by some brilliant stroke of luck. But I don't believe in coincidence. No, this feels too . . . intentional. It's not until we're almost at the last bend that I realize why.

A large group of harpies stand around squawking at each other as they guard a cave-in blocking the way forward. Smoke filters out from the holes in the broken earth and stones. Screams, coughing, and snarls cry out from the other side. They aren't blocking the way into the armory—they're blocking the way out. They've trapped the others inside and have set fire upon them. I'm so caught by the horror of what the harpies have done that I react a second too slow when one flies out of the shadows beside me, a guard in wait for others to fall into their trap. Its wolfsbane dipped claws drive forward to gut me but I'm shoved aside at the last second. I hit the floor hard and flip back up to find Alex to have taken the blow instead. Blood drips from his side as he sinks his teeth into the harpy's neck.

Other harpies take notice of the struggle behind them and turn about with their claws extended. I bark at Alex to get him moving. He struggles to rush after me but somehow he manages. We turn back the way we came and duck into one of the recovery rooms. I slam the door shut with my shoulder and swipe a paw to lock it. I know I've just thrown us into a corner but Alex is too injured to have made a proper run for it. The harpies ram the door from the other side and I know it's not going to last long.

"Genna . . ."

I turn away from the door to find Alex propped up

against the wall as his human self. Both hands are braced across his ribs on his left side. I shift a moment later and crouch next to him to inspect the damage.

"It's too late," he wheezes. "I can feel it in my blood."

No. I refuse to accept this. Not now. "You can fight this."

He struggles for breath and I struggle right along with him. He stretches out a shaky hand covered in his own blood. I take it in my own.

"There's no cure," he says between gasps. "Once it's in you, you're dead."

I shake my head. I can't accept that. There must be something more I can do.

"Save them," he says as the strength of his grip lessens by the second. "Save them all."

"I will." I don't know what else to say. I can only hold his hand and offer false promises as the harpies pound on the door. "I'll save them."

He coughs and blood paints his lips. "*All* of them. Remember . . . Rusty Dusty . . ."

Not just the ones smothering to death here and now. All of the lost souls led astray by Dasc.

With a faint smile, he runs one bloody finger down my nose. "Remember."

He knew. He noticed the sign James and I use in defiance of Dasc but he said nothing. He kept our secret. Here and now I at last find another ally only to lose him.

"I will. I will."

I repeat the words over and over again until his eyes stop looking at me but see somewhere far beyond. The world turns a hazy shade as tears pool in my eyes before falling to the dirty floor.

The beast always present on the inside begs to be unleashed to avenge this defeat. But the fur never comes, the fangs don't grow, my limbs don't contort. This pain spearing through my chest is the pain of Genna Barnes, not Genna the wolf.

But the wolf isn't the only beast inside me.

I rise to my feet as harpy claws manage to break through part of the door and stretch hopefully inside to swipe at the empty air. I can't defeat them as a wolf, not with those claws. But I can end them all as Genna Barnes—the lost daughter of Jefferson and Andromeda Barnes, the girl warrior, the heir apparent to a dark legacy, and the last hope any of us have.

With gentle fingers I close Alex's eyes and stand to find the hidden compartment in the wall. The armory isn't the only place that houses weapons as the foolish harpies think. Every room holds the means to defend ourselves. I dig at the dirt and stone as the harpies throw themselves against the door until I find what I'm looking for. My hand pulls free wrapped around the hilt of a heavy sword inlaid with faint lines of copper, bronze, silver, and shards of iron. The killer of a hundred monsters grasped in hand, I face the failing door without fear.

For it is them who should be afraid.

There are no heroes here. Only monsters.

The sword's gilded tip thrusts into the mass of flailing claws and arms. Screams fill my ears as I strike again and again until the door is clear. Unlatching the busted lock, I slip into the hallway as a shadowy wraith of pain and rage. The harpies are many and I am one but in my fierce onslaught, their bravery gives way to fear. The boldest of them manages to snag my long hair. Cutting myself free of my weakness with a snarl, a large chunk of my hair falls along with the harpy's foolish claws. The other harpies with their wolfsbane claws fail to reach me before meeting the sharp edge of my blade. I don't give them a shred of mercy and cut them down if they flee or if they stand against me. It doesn't matter. One by one they fall. The hallway behind me fills with the dead and fills before me with those about to join them. A few surviving werewolves manage to stagger out of their hiding places to join me but give me a wide berth as well.

Black blood drips from my hands, slides off my sword, and soaks my clothes. I truly am a wraith of terror.

The little girl who chased invisible monsters on her bicycle with a wooden sword has been forgotten. She doesn't exist here in this place, in my skin.

Hacking my way through the harpies I reach the blocked tunnel to the armory where smoke still puffs out. The sounds of howls and barking on the other side have quieted. Two others that joined me have been fighting with shovels in hand and use them to ferociously dig at the dirt and stones trapping our friends inside. I join them with my hands until my hands turn to paws to work faster. The four of us dig and dig, paws and hands turning raw and bloody from sharp rocks, until we make a hole and widen it enough so one of us can slip inside. A gust of smoke escapes from the hole and fills the entire tunnel ahead.

Shifting back, I rip off the bottom of my shirt and wrap it—blood soaked side facing out—around my mouth and nose. Not wasting a second, I slip through the hole and to the other side. One of my companions, Rosalyn, passes me my sword before following after. My eyes sting in the acrid haze. I blink away what I can of the smoke and continue on. Werewolves and friends lay on the floor, some still faintly coughing or struggling to escape. I gesture to Rosalyn to follow me while the other two remain behind to widen the hole. For once, Rosalyn doesn't question me and obeys without a word. We immediately start dragging people one by one to the exit. I don't bother checking to see who's still alive and who's not. I'm getting them all out. I'm going to save them.

Some still have life in them and do what little they can to help. And despite telling James and Kelsey to run to the Werewood, they reappear to help as well. The fires are stamped out and the injured carried to safety. As for the remaining harpies, I crawl out of a hole they made to the surface and hunt them down one by one as a hungering shadow in the darkness. If any try to escape, I follow them into the woods. I am not kind and I am not merciful. When at last the remaining are slain and the tip of my sword drags across the ground in my tired hand, I return to the compound to do what I can for the survivors. Dirt and blood smudged faces turn away and keep their eyes down. We've been defeated in our home. Our Whisper is dead. Many of our friends were slaughtered.

And where's Dasc? The man who proclaims he will keep us safe, who saved us from the horrors of the outside world? Who is nowhere to be found in our darkest hour?

After what happened, the wolves around me—as they cough with their smoke choked lungs and lick their wounds—don't ask for Dasc. They don't sit assured of his return. They don't pray to his godlike visage that he's shoved down our throats.

But they do call for me. They lower their eyes in respect. They give me their thanks. They reach out to touch my hands when I pass. I don't know how to feel or react. I just keep on moving and pulling bodies out of the compound. A shadow falls in step behind me to help my weary hands lift our fallen and toss the harpies into the few fires still raging. When my feet begin to stumble, my shadow gently grasps my arm to pull me to a halt.

"James." I say his name on a worn breath.

He doesn't say anything but slowly comes about so he can give me a hug. I don't melt in his arms or let myself crumble at this act of kindness. The things that once made me soft have been reforged into steel. Right now I can't feel anything past the pain lingering in my limbs. When I don't hug him back, he draws away and studies my face. I don't know what he sees there, but the sadness in his face only grows. He takes a step back. Then another.

"Whisper," he murmurs.

The word travels to everyone around us sitting above the smoking compound with the rising fire breaching the shallow halls. The title passes like fire of its own until it grows and is chanted back to me. My blood chills as they raise their voices and the path before me cements into stone.

"Whisper."

April 16, 2010
Day 4,915

I knew that this day would be coming sooner or later. I've played every card I have to postpone it with excuses that sound legitimate to Dasc. For the last year, ever since that attack on our previous compound, each time Dasc has come round he's been anxious and urging preparations for war to move at a faster pace. And part of that "preparation" is another Gathering of young children to fill in our ranks, especially since we lost so many in the harpy attack. But I've made sound arguments every time he brings it up—our new compound isn't completed yet. We don't have enough resources to accommodate a wave of children. We still need to figure out how the harpies found us in the first place, whether that be lax security measures or a mole on the inside.

But I've run out of ways to stall. Our new compound

near the mountains in the Canadian wilderness is even better than our last one—thanks to my very particular requests in order to drag out the construction of the tunnels and rooms. Our stores of provisions, weapons, and other commodities are full. We even learned that the harpies discovered us because one of the vampires that passed through the area had told them—before Kelsey tore him to pieces. Though part of me still wonders if Dasc was behind it. It wouldn't be the first time he's had monsters hurt us. The only thing now is to bolster our numbers that have greatly dwindled. Of those of us that are left, a third are getting "out of prime shape" as Dasc says. He wants fresh blood and he wants it now.

I go to wait at the southern entrance for Dasc's arrival. Not surprisingly, I find Rosalyn there as well. She doesn't even look in my direction but stands with her arms crossed over her chest and a sour, pinched look to her face. Everyone seems to be happy with me as their Whisper except for her. I'm sure she wanted the job for herself and is still working to impress Dasc. However, when she tried to do so by undermining me, Dasc chewed her out in front of everybody. Now she does anything I ask without hesitation as she tries to get back into his good graces again. Part of me takes pleasure in bossing her around. The other part aches for her twisted delusions in trying to earn the favor of the man that kidnapped us.

Right on time, the sentries open the hidden door and Dasc walks in as a giant black wolf. His yellow eyes lock onto me and I smile. It's genuine, though not for the reasons he suspects. I don't smile at his presence—I smile imagining killing him and seeing those yellow eyes lifeless. It's not a happy thought but it sure is satisfying.

He shifts between one step and the next to greet us on two feet, a crooked smile on his face. My smile widens as I imagine stabbing him in the neck and that stupid expression of his wilting into shock and pain.

"How are my girls?" he asks. He wraps me in a hug as if I truly do belong to him. Rosalyn scowls over his shoulder and waits for her turn but he ignores her.

"Things are going well," I say.

We walk step in step down the hallway, the tunnels wider and taller than the others I had grown used to in my old prison.

"How goes our call for allies?" Dasc asks and gives me his full attention. As usual, he seems on edge and he fidgets with his hands clasped behind his back.

"James came back last night after talking with the vampires," I say. "They're still in line, and Susan should be returning from the shapeshifters this evening."

Dasc nods and makes a disappointed hum under his breath. "Still not enough. We need more bodies."

More cannon fodder, he means. More werewolves to be cornered and slain.

"You still don't think the harpy attack was a singular incident?" I ask.

He shakes his head. "The war's coming. Soon. That was just a taste of what's ahead. We have to be prepared."

By turning and kidnapping more children to shove them in harm's way.

"We'll be ready," Rosalyn cuts in.

Dasc gives her a cold stare and she drops her gaze to the floor. He wraps an arm around my shoulders and says, "We have things to discuss in private before I receive a report from the others."

"Of course."

Without a backwards glance at Rosalyn, we continue down the hallway—all the while I have the urge to break Dasc's arm—until we reach what has been designated as the war room. A big circular table stands in the middle surrounded by chairs and lined with maps. A gasoline generator is tucked in the back in case we need it to run electronic equipment. Once inside, I shut the door behind us while Dasc slowly walks around the table inspecting the various maps.

"I take it things have been progressing well?" he asks. He slides his eyes up to me and remains there until I nod. His attention returns to the papers on the table. "Good. I could use a bit of good news."

"Then I assume the news you're bringing with you isn't good."

"It's not." He shakes his head sadly and sinks into one of the chairs to temple his fingers together, lost in thought. "Things are moving in the quiet and I fear we will not be prepared when the silence finally breaks."

I take a chair near him and lean forward with a frown. I always aim to look, sound, and act the part of the loyal disciple. I am concerned, that's not an act, but not out of fear for Dasc and his plans but what this news might mean for mine.

He sets his chin atop his templed fingers. "I've heard rumors of ancient things awakening and of tremors in an island near Greece. The very same island where Echidna supposedly died some centuries ago."

My muscles go rigid and I clench my jaw. Bad news indeed.

"There's word of leviathans again," Dasc continues. "Possibly hydra. It's Echidna, I know it, but she's moving carefully. She's smart, that one. She's learned from her mistakes. And the world's changed. I'm sure she'll find the best way to use it to her advantage."

A majestic class dragon rising out of the pits of the earth to crush us all. I've been warned about it for years, been taught to fight in the upcoming battle, but it was always some distant thing. The harpies made it a sharp reality but still . . .

"What can we do against such power?" I ask. "The werewolves alone can't face a threat like that. And even if we gather the vampires and shifters, it still won't be enough, not against the ancient ones."

"True. Which is why I've been mulling over other possibilities."

I don't think I like the sound of that at all. "Such as?"

"Unlikely allies. Or at least, useful if not entirely friendly powers to throw in Echidna's direction." He sits forward to rest his elbows on the table. "I have an associate who's been following age old clues to find certain gifted individuals that have fallen off the map. I believe these individuals could be persuaded to join the fight."

There's only one group of individuals he could be talking about. "The Magi." Men and women who drank of majestic dragon blood, becoming powerful enough to make even the majestics themselves afraid.

He smiles. "Excellent deduction, you clever girl."

"You think they're still alive?"

"Oh, yes. They may be forgotten—or covered up by Draco's lackeys—but I have no doubt they still live. And if we could persuade them to come out of the shadows once more, they could be very useful tools."

Not allies. Things to be used.

"But the Magi were created to combat Echidna's monsters," I say. "They would destroy us, not help us."

He rubs his chin thoughtfully and stares off into space. "Perhaps. Perhaps not. The world knows the power we werewolves possess. They know what we did to Echidna, to Terra. A power like that cannot be ignored. They'll need us to win this war. We are the key, Genna. Without us, the world will fall. It's our destiny to end Echidna for good, no matter the cost. We're not the menace. We're the salvation."

I consider that for a moment. He's right about the power in our bite. It stopped Echidna and made Terra a hapless dragon with little power left. The magic in us can stop majestic dragons and will be the best defense against Echidna's horde of monsters. The IMS doesn't realize how valuable we are to the war. It's our abilities that have thrown us to the forefront of the battle and why Echidna has set her eyes on us. We're the key to her undoing. Of course Echidna never realized that would be the case when she forcibly turned Dasc into the first of the werewolves—that we would be the ones to take her down.

I believe all of it. I've seen the monsters hunt us because we aren't one of them. We stand apart. Then the IMS hunts us because we *are* monsters but not the ones they should be fighting. We should be working together.

I'll fight in the coming war to protect the people under my charge, but I won't go looking for battle. No, the only fight I'll be seeking is the one that ends Dasc for good, because whether or not the werewolves are the key to saving the world, he won't be alive to see the end of it. He'll be dead by my hand first.

"We still need more soldiers," Dasc continues.

"We need more weapons in our arsenal," I counter. "Has your associate been successful in finding any of the Magi?"

"He has." He looks a bit smug as he says it. "He's managed to avoid the eye of the dragons as well. Draco has no idea what we've been up to. When the time is right, we will call upon the Magi, force them from hiding if we have to."

I still can't imagine how he'll be able to get them on our side and not kill us instead. From the stories I've been told, they are wild and powerful, beings that none could control.

Dasc gets up from his seat and stretches his arms towards the ceiling. "It's been a long journey."

I rise as well. "Your quarters have been prepared for you. Once Susan returns, I'll inform you and gather the others."

He swaggers over and claps a hand on my shoulder. "That's my girl."

I want to break every single one of his fingers.

He leaves the room and I'm left to ponder the news he brought. I sit as a spider on the edge of a very tangled web, judging which strings to carefully tug on to get what I want—the safety of the werewolves and the death of Dasc. Every path I might choose is dangerous and guarded by enemies on every side. If I don't convince the werewolves to join me, then they'll join the ranks of enemies too. If I don't play my cards just right, Dasc could kill me. If I do nothing at all, the IMS or the monsters could kill us all. What a very tangled web indeed.

I sit and stare at the maps on the table as I debate how the Magi fit into the grand scheme of things. If Dasc tries to use them as tools, perhaps I could instead persuade them to be my allies against him.

"I thought I'd find you here."

James walks into the room and takes the seat next to me. I figured he'd come find me sooner or later. He's gotten so tall over the years, and that boyish face of his has transformed into that of a man—the beard certainly helps with that. He's not a runt of a kid anymore. He's my comrade in arms, my confidant, my brother. But even now with all his brawn from relentless training, I still see him as someone to protect. I promised to get us both home one day. I haven't forgotten.

"So?" he prompts.

I hoist my feet up to rest them crossed on top of the table. "Dasc is seeking out the Magi and wants to use them in the war ahead."

James leans back in his chair. "Huh."

"And he wants more soldiers."

We share a meaningful look. We both know we're running out of time. If we reach the point where Dasc kidnaps more children, we won't play pretend anymore. We'll refuse and save those children. But doing so would also put our families in danger. Our edge over Dasc could be lost. So we need to kill Dasc before it comes to that while we have the element of surprise. Then there's the other part of the puzzle we can't ignore. We need Dasc in order to find the other werewolf compounds. If we can't find them, then we can't liberate them. And if we can't liberate them, then the cycle continues on and on.

A tangled web where any choice we make could have dire consequences. We must tread so very, very carefully, especially with Dasc near again.

There's a light knock on the door and my oldest sentry Mark steps in. "Whisper, we need your guidance at the southern gate."

James looks to me with raised eyebrows. "That doesn't sound good."

"I'm on my way." Sliding my feet off the table, I follow Mark down the halls I just walked with Dasc to the southern entrance. James tags along behind curiously. We walk through the secret door and out into the wilderness beyond. This particular route into the compound is covered by winding trees and sharp rock precipices—a highly defensible position and well hidden. Outside I find Susan waiting wrapped in a worn jacket with a tattered backpack on her shoulder.

"I wasn't expecting you until this evening," I say.

She shoots a glance at Mark and James. She seems on edge, wary, and her blonde hair flies free in a wispy storm to make her look even more unbound. "I finished early, and I came across something on my way back that you need to see. I need a Whisper's guidance."

Susan's spooked by something, there's no doubt about that. I've rarely, if ever, seen her this way. She's always so stoic and strong. I've come to depend on her and made her one of my close advisors. If there's anyone that cares about the safety of the wolves themselves, it's Susan. And if she's worried about something now, then I should be worried too.

"Watch the gate," I tell Mark. He bobs his head and slips inside to seal the door. I give James a meaningful look too. He backtracks unwillingly after Mark. With the entrance shut, it blends seamlessly into the tangled roots and rocks.

"This way." Susan sets off without waiting for a response and marches down the slippery rocks.

I jog after her with sure feet and into the winding wood. We walk and walk and walk until Susan stops dead in the middle of the forest and cocks her head to listen intently to our surroundings. I do the same but it's clear there's no one else around. We're alone.

"Dasc has returned?" she asks. I nod. She licks her lips and starts to fiddle with the strap of her pack. "I should have come back sooner."

"Susan, what's going on?"

She starts to pace back and forth like a trapped animal. Even though I'm not in wolf form, I can feel my hackles start to rise. Eventually Susan swings about abruptly and grasps both of my hands in her own.

"I tried to do my best," she says. "I tried to take care of you and protect you. You know that, don't you?"

My eyes narrow. Something must be very wrong. "Susan."

"I did what I could with what little control I had," she continues. "I wasn't a Whisper and was never going to be one. That was clear to me straight off. So I did what I could. I tried to be there for you and the other children."

"What's going on?"

She shakes her head with a grimace. A person who didn't know her might think her mad. I, however, see the distress and despair. I return the grip on her hands and tug her a little as if to shake some sense into her. Her head snaps up.

"We can't do another Gathering. We can't."

I blink. Susan, the ever loyal soldier to Dasc, doesn't want to follow his order to bolster our ranks?

"This has all been madness," she whispers and draws me close so our faces are a foot apart. "I learned things, Genna. The shapeshifters know far more than I think even Dasc realizes."

That certainly gets my attention. "What do they know?"

"The truth—about the werewolves, about the war, about Dasc. All of it. And they told me so I could try to put a stop to it. But I can't do it without you. I need you to listen to me. Please. Just listen."

"You always have my ear, you know that."

She nods but doesn't start talking immediately. I know that fear in her face, the fear that somehow word will get back to Dasc and she'll be punished. It's a twisted truth that none of us can truly trust each other—none of us that want to be free any way. Dissension is not tolerated.

"Our purpose is a lie," she whispers. "The war is a lie. We're not soldiers to save the world. We're tools in a vendetta. And the horrors of the serum are a lie. There's a power out there that could save us but Dasc has keep it secret, buried it in blood."

My pulse thunders in my ears and my grip tightens on her hands. "Are you saying—?"

"There's a chance for a cure but Dasc has kept it from us so he can seek his own revenge."

"Revenge?"

"Against Echidna. He wasn't forcibly turned, Genna. He—"

"My my, what are you two gossiping about?"

We spin about to find Dasc striding up to us with his hands in his pockets looking utterly at ease except for the fact his eyes are blazing yellow.

It's only with years of practice that I'm able to keep breathing. We've been caught red-handed just as Susan manages to find some of the most damning evidence yet. The potential for a cure that he's withheld from us. A conspiracy about the approaching war. The truth about Dasc's history. We've been caught. I was too lax. I should have been more aware, but of course he could sneak up on us. It's him. He's a living blind spot when he wants to be.

As he stalks towards us, I can see my years of hard work crumbling into dust. Whatever happens next, it ends with his secrets remaining hidden and us most likely dead.

"I asked what you're gossiping about," he says and comes to a stop five feet away.

I try to think of a way to maneuver out of this but I can't see a path that leads to both me and Susan walking away alive. I could feign innocence and profess loyalty but that would leave Susan on her own. If Dasc attacks, I will step in to save her so it will be over for me any way.

While I scheme in the breathless seconds, Susan's face hardens and she steps forward.

"I just learned some damning truths from my recent outing, Dasc. Or should I say Lycaon?"

The intense yellow in his eyes flares.

"Oh?" he says calmly even though his body language says he's anything but calm. "And what exactly did you learn, my dear Susan?"

Her hands curl into fists even as her hands shake. I stand next to her tense as a bow string. A fight is coming.

"How about the fact that you've been lying to us about the serum?" she says. "I know where the serum comes from. There's a Magus out there with the ability to calm the disease. And if he exists, then there's every chance that another Magus could cure us. The power is out there but you'd rather snuff it out, make us afraid of it, then try to help us."

He cocks his head to the side. "And I suppose a shapeshifter told you this? Some lie to turn you against me?"

"It's not a lie." She rolls back her sleeve to show a needle mark at the crook of her elbow. "I took it. It's not pain, it's freedom."

"You may think that, but the same is not true for everyone."

"That's a lie!" She shouts. "And even if it wasn't, you still aren't saving us. You turned us! Maybe you convinced the others to forget but I haven't! You didn't show up and take us away to a safe place. You turned all of us. Made us your pawns."

He clenches his jaw. Susan knows. She knows everything. Another ally has been under my nose without my knowing. Just like Alex.

"You're confused," Dasc says. "I didn't ask this for any of you. I saved you, just like I had to save myself."

"Except that Echidna didn't force you to become a werewolf," she says bravely in the face of Dasc's growing rage. "You volunteered. You worshipped her. You *asked* to drink her blood and become what you are. But when you wanted to turn your family too, she killed them. She didn't want to share her play things."

I don't know if Dasc is still breathing. My body trembles as I wait for him to attack. I'll fight him off if I have to. If Susan can escape, she can get to James and safety. Perhaps somehow they can convince the others of the truth Susan has learned. As for me...I knew sacrifices needed to be made. I just didn't expect I'd be one of them.

"This war isn't about saving us from Echidna," Susan continues and shakes her head with disgust. "It's about taking revenge for your family. You ripped us from ours so you could use us to get you close enough to kill her."

"Choose your next words carefully," he says with lethal calm.

But Susan—head-strong and unrelenting Susan—says, "I wonder what your dead wife Selene would think of the monster you've become. Or your daughter Phaedra. I heard Echidna was not kind when she—"

Faster than I can blink, Dasc launches at Susan and sinks his human teeth into her throat. A second. That's all it takes between Susan standing there alive and challenging Dasc on everything he is . . . and falling to the ground with her throat ripped out.

I can't move. I can hardly think. My body is frozen as if my will isn't my own anymore.

Dasc spits out blood and flesh, panting hard. He stands over Susan's unmoving corpse for a long moment until he turns to me. Blood coats his mouth, chin, and dribbles down his neck.

The black wolf was never the beast. This is the true monster.

"I had to do that," he says in a gravelly voice.

His yellow eyes are near hypnotic as I sway where I stand.

"She was pulling a hidden knife and about to attack us."

A knife? What knife?

Dasc steps closer. But I can't move.

"I had to stop her. The shapeshifters fed her lies and turned her against us."

Lies?

"Nothing she said is important. Forget what she said. You trust me, don't you?"

His voice echoes in my head like a thousand drums. Trust?

A sense of warmth wraps around me despite the horror at my feet. The yellow eyes watching me are not to be feared. No, of course not. They're full of sorrow for what he had to do. He didn't want this. Susan forced his hand.

I trust him. I've always trusted him. How couldn't I?

Dizzy and disoriented, I sway and stumble to the side.

"Susan . . ." I breathe. The smell of death overtakes my senses and my stomach roils.

"I'm so sorry," he says and steps closer holding his hands out towards me. "I'll protect you. I'll always protect you. You know that, don't you?"

I stare at him and the blood on his face. I'm not afraid. There's an ache in my chest I can't ignore. Stepping forward carefully, I embrace Dasc and he cups the back of my head. I'm safe here.

"I'd do anything for you," he whispers at my ear. "And you'd do the same for me, wouldn't you?"

My reply is automatic. "Yes."

"No one is to hear the lies Susan brought here. Do you understand?"

"Yes."

"That's my girl."

I look away from Susan and the gore. She had become my surrogate mother. She protected me and held my hand and—

She betrayed us. Yes. That's right. Dasc saved me. Saved us all.

"I'll take care of this. Just wait here."

I nod and remain where I am staring glassy eyed ahead. In my peripheral vision, I see Dasc drag Susan's limp body over the edge of the rocks and toss her. There's several heavy thumps before a noisy splash as her corpse hits the stream below. Dasc returns to my side and throws an arm over my shoulders.

"Everything's going to be okay. I'll stay with you for a while and make sure we're all safe. Would you like that?"

"Yes."

"Good."

We walk together step in step away from the scene of that horrible betrayal. My mind slips away into a dark corner as we return to the compound and I everything I do becomes robotic. There's no feeling apart from a sense of security with Dasc always lingering at my side. I do things because I'm supposed to do them. It's my duty. I assure the other werewolves. I tell them not to go looking for Susan and to leave her lie. I tell them that Dasc will take care of everything. We are safe here. The shapeshifters that attempted to betray us will be dealt with swiftly.

For days I languish in a fog. Dasc is in my every thought, every motion, every compulsion to do anything. He cares for me. I care for him. We're family. When he smiles at me, I smile back. I vaguely notice James looking sad and uncomfortable but I can't imagine why. Dasc saved us. We owe him because we're family.

It's a rare treat for Dasc to stay with us for so long. A week passes and then another. He's always at my side—to give me support.

Then he leaves to go hunting and promises to return. I wait patiently in the war room until he can return. An hour passes. Then another.

A chill enters my blood as his presence begins to fade.

Susan.

A gasp sticks in my throat and I choke on it.

Susan.

My empty emotions come flooding back without Dasc's influence to keep me on a tight leash. I heave a dry sob and cover my mouth with my hands.

Everything in my mind is a confusing mess of conflict but one image remains crystal clear—Susan's body at my feet as I did nothing. She came and told me lies about Dasc. Or . . . did she? What really happened? I know Dasc was there and he saved me. But . . . why? What did he save me from?

I grasp at my hair and take fast shallow breaths.

The door to the room opens and I can't collect myself fast enough when I whip about to see who it is.

James shuts the door behind him and gives me a long look.

When I give another dry sob, we stride for each other and I clutch onto him as I cry silently into his shoulder to stifle the sound. James just holds onto me and strokes my hair. As Dasc's presence continues to wane, my thoughts become clear until I realize just what's happened. I've been under his spell of persuasion ever since he killed Susan in order to make sure I'd stay in line. This hunting expedition of his is undoubtedly a test to see what I'll do without his presence to keep me in check. Meaning he's going to come back. Meaning I have to pretend I don't want to tear his eyes out, rip his heart from his chest, and leave him for the crows like he did Susan.

I've been a puppet on strings, unable to mourn, unable to fight. Powerless.

Never before have I hated the disease in my veins more. Never have I hated *him* more.

"He made me watch," I whisper and push away from James as confusion and grief give way to absolute fury.

"*He made me watch!*"

I grab the edge of the table and flip it with an almighty roar. Maps and papers scatter, chairs go tumbling, and I want to smash everything to bits. Before I can do anything, James grabs my arm. I turn about snarling but he holds steadfast, deep shadows under his eyes.

"He'll know," is all he says.

My arms fall lifeless to my sides.

"I don't even know what's real or not anymore," I breathe and take a shaky breath.

"I'm real."

We hold each other's gaze for a long time until together, despondently, we righten the table, pick up the maps and papers, and set up the chairs until it looks just the way it had been. Soon I can feel the pinpricks of Dasc thoughts coming for me again.

"Don't let me forget," I whisper. "Don't *ever* let me forget, no matter what he does."

"Never."

Taking the utmost care, I settle back into my chair to wait once again. James slips away and while alone, I steel myself for the tests ahead. For once, I don't know if I'll have the patience to see this through without trying to kill him first.

Dasc enters the room and I turn about to find him, robotic once again as if I never snapped out of his poisonous grasp.

"How went the hunt?" I ask, my voice flat and even.

He studies me for a long moment before a smile touches his lips. "It went well. Come. You can help me with the meal."

I follow him into the kitchens where he's hauled his catch—a large buck—and has me assist in gutting it. It's almost impossible for my hand not to shake as I grip the knife. I can imagine flipping it around and plunging it into Dasc's heart. He knows it too. This is yet another test in his macabre game.

What I feel for Susan and her murder, I tuck away into the furthest reaches of my mind. I am a ghost and feel nothing. I tell myself that over and over again. I'm already dead on the inside. I cannot feel. I will not feel.

Dasc stays another week but doesn't use his force of persuasion on me for the duration. Another test to see if I'll crack and expose the anger boiling underneath or the homicidal tendencies I have to fight off at any given moment. I let him linger beside me. I let him put his hands on my shoulders. I let him live.

But I pass. At the end of the week, he proclaims he has to seek out other allies. He parts after forcing one last hug on me. Just before he goes, I see him glance over my shoulder and pause a second long enough to make me wonder. When he finally vanishes, I turn around to find Rosalyn walking away. And just like that, I know Dasc will still have his eyes watching me while he's away.

I wait a day. Then another. When Rosalyn is asleep and I know Dasc is truly gone, I slip away into the night with James at my side. In the darkness, we hunt the sharp rocks, stone crevices, and all along the banks of the stream until we find where Dasc left Susan to rot. I try not to breathe or even look as we gather what remains of my guardian. With careful hands, we wrap her in a linen I took from the compound and lay her in a grave dug by our own paws. And under the moonlight, we send Susan off to her forever rest beneath a blanket of warm earth, leaves, and grass. We leave no stone to mark her grave or marker of any kind lest Dasc or Rosalyn find it.

When the work is done and our hands are covered in dirt, we stand side by side to say our own silent farewells. A nightly breeze wraps around us and I let my last tears fall with my mind clear. There were so many things I should have said to her, so many things I wish I had known about her. She didn't deserve her fate. She didn't deserve this life.

I kneel in the dirt and press my palm to the soil.

"Be free," I whisper.

And wish that I could be free too.

June 7, 2010
Day 4,967

Standing outside the small, nondescript cabin hidden amongst the woods—a remote IMS outpost—I start to wonder if I placed my trust in the wrong person. Then again, it isn't trust really. It's odds. The odds are good that this particular shapeshifter who managed to escape Dasc's wrathful cleansing wants him dead as much as I do. She's provided useful information thus far—of course, in exchange for what information I have on Dasc's movements. It's a gamble, but every step I've taken so far in my life has been a risk. This is a gamble worth taking and a golden opportunity I couldn't pass up when we stumbled across each other while both assessing IMS movements in the area. She wanted my help. I wanted her help. And so far Dasc doesn't have a clue what we've been up to.

Zeredah steps out of the IMS outpost in the guise of one

of its agents. She's a clever shapeshifter and knows when to be who at exactly the right moment. It's a useful skill that not all shapeshifters have. She strides to me in a heavy overcoat and documents in hand. She passes the papers over when she reaches me and rolls her shoulders.

"It's the best I could do on short notice," she says. "It'll get you in, but landing is going to be the real problem."

My eyes narrow on the unassuming shapeshifter. "I thought you were going to walk us through security."

"Normally I would, but not with Dasc sniffing this close. Besides, werewolves are the only ones the French will shoot on sight. The risk's too great for me."

"I don't like last minute changes in plan. Makes you appear . . . rather untoward."

She smiles. "I'm a shapeshifter, love. I'm always untoward." She raps a finger on the papers in my hand. "Just make sure you get out of there as fast as you can. France is a dangerous place."

"I'm a dangerous person."

"I know. Which is why they'll shoot you on sight." She rolls her shoulders and clears her throat. "Look, I wouldn't normally say this but I've grown a tad fond of you, so don't take any unnecessary risks. Take my advice. Despite whatever opportunities may arise, go see my friend there first. Don't rush for Erebus at the first sign."

I glower at her. "I don't rush into anything. And I know how to be careful."

She rolls her eyes and mutters, "Geez, I show a little compassion once in my life and have it thrown back in my face."

Deciding not to comment, I turn and head into the

forest. It's time to move. Dasc has called me to Europe to deal with what he would only say is "a sticky situation." I'm bringing James along. It also so happens that Zeredah's "friend" overseas heard word that Erebus—Dasc's associate locating the Magi—is in the same area we're headed. If we can get to him, find out about the Magi, we might locate some new allies or even a cure.

Then a gruff male voice calls out behind me. "Genna."

I freeze and ice chills my veins. Stiffly I turn about to find Zeredah to be replaced by a face that I've only seen in my dreams since I was seven. Time may have ravaged my memories but I know that face. I have the same eyes, the same stubborn look, and have tried to achieve the same countenance.

My father.

My father dressed in the same heavy overcoat Zeredah had been wearing when she looked like a woman mere moments ago.

Knowing that it's Zeredah under that mask of a face, I want to punch my fist through her spleen. I also know that shapeshifters can't just pick faces out of thin air. She's seen him, been face to face.

"What are you playing at?" I say, making my warning clear with the intonation of my words.

"I wanted to see how you would react," the shapeshifter says, wearing my father's face and speaking with his voice. "This . . . *form* is probably the greatest shock I could produce, but you reacted splendidly. Didn't jump or act surprised at all."

"Which proves what exactly?"

My father walks forward and the ache in my chest swells

until it's too painful to breathe. But I've lived my life in deceit and lies. Keeping up the pretense of being unaffected comes more naturally now than actually showing any emotions buried beneath.

He smiles and lays a hand on my shoulder. I don't make a move but for one very small moment I let myself imagine it really is him—until the iron doors in my brain snap shut on that ridiculous notion.

"I wanted to know if you could fool *him*," the mimic of my father says.

"Satisfied?"

"Very."

"Then get your hand off my shoulder."

He withdraws but the smile doesn't fade from his face.

Before I can change my mind, I ask, "When did you see him?"

The lines in his face sharpen as his eyelids crinkle. "Not too long ago."

"How was he?"

"Tired. Worn. Alive. And still looking for you."

After all this time . . . he hasn't given up on me.

"You know, I think the wolves are lucky to have you," my father's shadow says. "Very lucky indeed."

"I'm so glad to have your approval," I say flatly.

"You're not a fool, Genevieve Barnes. And you're not Dasc's fool either. You may be the most competent rebel your kind has had in a long time. Perhaps good enough to turn the tables. Good luck, Dark Whisper."

Unable to look at that face any longer, I walk away from the reminder of what I've lost and what I'm still fighting for.

Five minutes later I find James waiting for me with a

pack slung over his shoulder and another at his feet. As soon as I come into view, he picks up the other bag and tosses it to me.

"Everything set?" he asks.

I nod. "You can still change your mind."

"Not a chance. No one goes lone wolf. You know what a bad idea that is."

"I still think you should stay and watch over the compound."

He readjusts the pack on his shoulder and waves a hand absently at me. "If worse comes to worse, Kelsey will step in."

"If Rosalyn doesn't stab him in the back first."

"Maybe. But I think she knows Kelsey would be too much of a fight."

"I know." I sling my bag onto my shoulder. "That's why I said she'd stab him in the back."

He shrugs and we walk along in silence for a while. The sound of the birds is subdued this morning as if they too know what is about to happen next. Everything we've gone through up until this point could hang in the balance.

"Genna?" James says quietly. "I want you to promise me something."

"What?"

"Promise that no matter what happens, at least one of us is going home."

"We're all making it home."

He holds an arm out in front of me and brings us both to a stop. "Genna, I mean it. We both know Dasc won't hesitate to kill either of us if he figures out what we're up to. But one of us has to go home."

"Either one of us."

"Exactly. If I snuff it, tell my parents I never stopped trying to get back home."

I swallow. It's something I don't want to think about. "Same goes for me."

"Promise?" He holds out his hand.

"Promise." I slip my fingers around his and give his hand a solid shake.

And just like that we're off. We locate the car Zeredah procured for us waiting at a nearby town already gassed up and ready to go. Following her instructions carefully, we make our way undetected through the airport in Toronto, go through security without a hitch, and then settle in for the long flight to Paris, France.

James and I sleep in rotating shifts. Even up here in an airplane, we're cautious. We have enemies on a number of sides, from IMS agents to Echidna's fiends to Dasc's most loyal followers.

As we rumble over the Atlantic and James takes his turn to sleep, I comb through everything in my head. I had received an urgent message from Dasc at the compound. We set up the generator and took his call on a satellite phone. He made us go through every single precaution we've ever conjured in order to make sure we were both who we said we were. He said nothing was safe anymore and that he needed me more than ever. He didn't dare risk saying too much over the phone except that he couldn't trust anyone where he was—which was Greece at the time. Something had gone terribly wrong, he said. The war was coming upon us and he ordered me to fly into France straight away. *France* of all places, where they either shoot or lock up werewolves on the spot.

And which also happens to be the last known location of Erebus, my elusive link to the Magi and a possible cure for the curse in my veins. Zeredah had her contacts in Europe keeping any eye out for him and trying to track his movements. He's good at hiding but that's to be expected of the man Dasc has entrusted to seek out the Magi for him. The only question is how to get to Erebus in a way that doesn't arouse suspicion? And what has happened that has thrown Dasc into a near panic?

We wait out the long hours of the flight until at last we descend to the airport on the outskirts of Paris. James and I walk out of the jetway and into the concourse, straight into a pair of security guards watching every single person getting off the plane. While they don't appear to be actively scanning or frisking anyone, I can see them each carrying devices in hand that they hold discreetly towards disembarking passengers. I'll bet anything they're IMS agents checking for magical individuals coming into the country. Both Zeredah and Dasc warned us about such precautions the French take. A lot of countries don't have the manpower or finances for such operations but the noble class dragons that rule the IMS here have deep pockets.

Taking a chance, I bend down to tie my shoe before reaching the security agents. James stands beside me looking rather bored as more of the passengers slip around us. While momentarily screened, I pull back my sleeve and bite my arm hard enough to draw blood. Straightening back up, I bump into another passenger and make sure to smudge some of the blood onto their jacket. I offer a quick apology and the woman mutters something irritably before passing on. When she walks between the two security guards, their devices must catch something because they make her pause. The second their attention is momentarily distracted, James and I slip behind them and into the throng of passengers heading for baggage pickup. We try to hurry without drawing too much attention. Those security guards are sure to realize that the woman isn't a werewolf but there's one bleeding nearby. We have to get out of this airport.

Security is everywhere and around every corner. James and I stick close to each other, watching the guards in our peripheral vision. A few of them listen to their walkie talkies and then start urgently searching the crowds. James tugs on my arm and we hasten through the terminal to a pair of elevators. The quick footsteps of security come up behind us. An elevator opens up ahead and we slip in, hit the button for the ground floor, and—just before two guards reach us—the doors close.

"They'll be waiting for us on the next stop," James says and rolls his shoulders.

"Yup." I hit the emergency stop button between floors and put my hands on the doors. "Time to get out."

With James helping me, we force open the doors half way between levels and startle several flyers waiting for the lifts. I pull myself up easy as you please and scan the floor for security. They haven't gotten here quite yet but it won't take them long. James clambers up beside me.

"*Excusez moi*," I say and cut through the waiting crowd.

Ripping open the zipper of my carry-on, I put on a hat as I walk swiftly and reverse the light jacket I'm wearing. James does the same beside me. Getting out of the airport becomes a dance of changing clothes, shifting speeds, and taking odd turns, even walking calmly back towards security guards in the confusion so we slip right past them. Eventually we make it to the waiting shuttle station. We pretend to hop on one bus only to walk straight through and out the rear exit much to the dismay of the driver. We do this once more before sneaking into the parking garage. Using skills we picked up during the last few years of our training with the werewolves, I break into a car while James keeps watch and then hotwire it. We need to get out of here and lay low until we're supposed to meet Dasc in the basement of a restaurant that runs a sort of underground railroad.

We clear the parking garage, exit the airport, and are flying high on success. James breathes a sigh of relief and gives me a tentative smile. Though things have gone relatively well so far, I know we can't let our guard down. The IMS security at the airport knows at least one werewolf has entered the country and I doubt they'll just let us go. They'll be hunting for us.

I don't let myself be distracted by the beautiful city around me as I drive in a car that I have to adapt to quickly. I don't think about the towering buildings, the small cobbled streets, the interesting people on the sidewalks, the delicious smells from bakeries and restaurants. I'm focused solely on getting to where we need to be and if anyone is following us. For such a bright, warm, sunny day, everything seems so dark to me. This is a city hell-bent on wiping people like me off the earth. There is cruelty and danger hiding beneath the beauty.

In fact, I don't let myself even think about why we're here until we finally reach a large public park where we stop and ditch the car. We walk through the trees, neatly trimmed fields, and glamorous gardens—that my gaze clings to with envy. After fifteen minutes we find what we're looking for.

"Over there," James says to me in an undertone. I look in the direction he nods to and spot the building between the trees and spectacular flower gardens—the Château de Bagatelle where Zeredah said her contact would be waiting for us. We have some time before we're supposed to meet Dasc at the restaurant. If this contact is as valuable as Zeredah insists, then we need to talk to this person, whoever they are.

We're so close.

Then the hairs stand up on the back of my neck as I sense movement in the shadows to our right. I glance out of the corner of my eye and duck just as a French IMS agent steps out from behind a tree and fires a bio-mech gun at us. James and I instinctively split off in two different directions to give him separate moving targets. While I race in the direction of the château, James runs at an angle towards the agent to draw his attention. After several yards I make a sharp turn, vault over some stones and roots, and come up to the agent from behind. Before he even knows I'm there, I've taken the gun out of his hands and flattened him to the ground.

There's bound to be more than one agent here. I don't know if they managed to follow us from the airport or if we stumbled right into an agent that somehow knows what we are.

James gasps beside me and I spin about to face whatever has snuck up on us. Before I can see who—or what—has come, the gun in my hand grows so hot that it burns my skin. I drop it with a start and jerk my head up to see who we have to face next.

A woman steps out from between rows of vibrant red roses. She holds no weapon but has a single hand outstretched towards us and my instant thought is that she's a magic wielder. Her youthful face, currently twisted in a look of loathing, is framed by volumes of white hair. She's dressed far better than I would expect any IMS agent to be and with a twist of her wrist, I feel snakes of white-hot fire wrap around my wrists and drag me down to the ground. I bite back my cry of pain as she walks ever closer. When she's only a few feet away, towering over James and me trapped on the ground, I see her icy blue eyes change shape into slits.

She's no Blessed. She's a dragon.

I should have seen it straight away after all of those history lessons I had with Alex. If I'm not mistaken, this dragon is one of the offspring in a powerful line of noble class dragons sired by Draco himself. Marked by the white hair and fire magic, I've no doubt she's one of Draco's kin.

"Celeste!" another woman shouts behind the dragon.

She drops her hand and the burning around my wrists disappears but her scowl remains. I consider making a run for it but I know such action would be futile. This dragon—Celeste, I assume—would have no trouble stopping us.

The woman who called out to the dragon appears from behind the rose bushes slightly out of breath, a bio-mech gun held in her hand. In plain clothes that look much more normal than the silk and brocade Celeste is wearing, I imagine this might actually be an IMS agent. The woman appears to start arguing with Celeste in rapid French as James and I kneel in the grass. They haven't killed us outright so that's something, but we've been caught. I glance to the château barely visible between the hedges and trees. We were so close, so damn close.

But this is no time to let anger and frustration overwhelm me. I'm a clever girl. There may yet be a way to maneuver out of this predicament.

After much arguing between the dragon and woman, the woman turns to us as she pulls out a pair of handcuffs.

In perfect English, the woman announces, "You are under arrest! Don't move or we will be forced to harm you."

I don't move as the agent pulls back my aching wrists to bind them. Two men show up during this time and one produces another set of cuffs for James. Once cuffed, we're pulled to our feet and escorted through the trees and gardens. Many eyes follow us as we pass families, bikers, and runners using the park. Celeste leads the way to a car parked not far from where James and I ditched the stolen car. We're stuffed into the back while the woman takes the driver's seat and Celeste sits in the front beside her.

Rumbling along to who knows where, I consider our options. Trying to battle a dragon head on is a bad idea, no matter what class they might be. We only have one weapon that works against dragons—the bite of a werewolf. If it comes to that, I'll use it, but I'd rather not. Since they haven't killed us yet as I was led to believe all Paris agents would, perhaps they can be reasoned with, even be made useful. I don't trust them, not by a long shot, but if they knew the truth about our background, perhaps they would help us. But would it be worth the risk telling them? Or would the best option be to do whatever we can to flee? If Dasc found out we consorted with them, he'd kill us and our families.

I think of the stories told to me growing up. Dragons are not to be trusted. They may be the champions of the IMS but they seek their own agendas above all others. We're nothing but grime to be wiped clean off the face of the Earth. And I still remember the attitude of the IMS agents I stumbled across in Canada. They found werewolves to be revolting things—not even to be considered people. How do I know that any IMS agent thinks differently? The only one I could truly trust would be my father, but as luck would have it, he's an ocean away.

Fleeing now would be pointless. They know we're here, what we look like, and I've no doubt this Celeste would call down the full power of her brood and the IMS in the area to find us. No, our best option is to be clever. I look to James and find he's waiting for me to come to some sort of decision. He covertly points to the door but I shake my head slightly. I tap a finger to my wrist to indicate that we wait.

Our captors drive for fifteen minutes and I count the turns, watch the street signs, and keep my bearings at all times to know exactly where we are. Out of the corner of my eye I spot James doing the same. On the plane ride here, I studied a map of Paris to learn the best escape routes and places to hide if need be. Not surprisingly, it comes in handy when we finally stop and I still know precisely where we are in the city. Celeste and the female agent pause to make sure there's no one paying attention before pulling us out of the car.

We've stopped in front of what appears to be an apartment building of some sort with iron-wrought railings on each balcony shaded with heavy red curtains. James and I are led inside to a small marble foyer that smells of lemon cleaner. Our captors don't linger in any spot for long as they guide us past the foyer, through a long hallway, up a flight of stairs, and to what could be a normal apartment. The female agent comes to a halt as if assessing the room. We've stopped in an open dining room with a kitchen on our right and bedrooms on either side.

"We should 'ave brought them to 'eadquarters," Celeste says testily.

The agent doesn't even look in her direction. "If we brought them to headquarters, they would have been shot on the spot. You're so focused on wiping them out, you fail to see any benefits in keeping them alive."

"And you fail to remember who's in charge 'ere."

"We both work for the IMS. Your family just has more money than mine."

Celeste snarls and the sound is distinctively not human. "Watch your tone."

"I think we should question them separately," the agent says, ignoring the threat. "I'll take the girl."

It's clear the dragon does not like being bossed around in the slightest. The temperature in the room shoots up a few degrees before she grabs James by the arm and hauls him into one of the bedrooms. I don't like us being separated.

"Take a seat." The agent pulls out a chair at the dining table.

I don't move. "Why are you doing this?"

"What?"

"Not killing us."

She sighs and gestures for me to take the chair again. I don't.

"There's a reason you came here," she says. "You seem like a smart person to me. You wouldn't come here—France of all places—without a reason. So, I find myself curious. And to be honest, I don't want to kill you or your friend. I find the French policy a bit . . . distasteful."

I watch her closely from her crossed arms to the unassuming face. She's nowhere as aggressive as her counterpart and she doesn't appear to be a native to the area.

"Where are you from?" I ask. "Not Paris I take it."

She tilts her head to the side considering me. "The States actually. I'm here for international communication studies. And despite the attitude towards werewolves in Europe, I've seen the other side of things. I know werewolves don't ask for this life. A lot of people fail to see the true victims in this whole mess. That's why I'd rather ask questions than go on a shooting spree, thank you very much."

After a moment, I sink into the offered seat. The agent smiles and pulls around another chair to sit across from me.

"I'm Agent Denworth," she says. "What's your name?"

Do I dare risk the chance of telling the truth here? If I tell an agent, then surely she could get word back to my father. At least he'd know I'm alive. But if Dasc somehow finds us and knows I said anything, he'll most likely kill my father. It's too great a risk. When I remain silent, the agent leans forward on her forearms.

"I'm trying to give you a chance here," she says quietly and glances towards the closed bedroom door. At least I haven't heard any raised voices or anything to suggest Celeste is hurting James. "You help me, and I can help you."

I'd like to believe it but I know trust is a double-edged sword.

With no answer forthcoming, Agent Denworth sighs and rubs her hands together. "Look, we know Dasc has made it into the country. Then suddenly you two show up. Don't tell me there isn't a connection."

He's here. I have the urge to glance over my shoulder to make sure he isn't peering in through a window or some nonsense.

"Help us catch him," the agent continues and rests a hand on my knee trying to plead with me. "We can't spring a trap unless we know where he's going. If you know that, if you can help lure him in, we can do the rest."

"You can't kill him," I say immediately.

"Don't underestimate our—"

"No, I mean, you need to keep him alive."

The agent drops her gaze and rolls her lips. "Look, I don't know what kind of hold he has over you but—"

"That's not it at all. I'd like to drown him in his own blood myself but he has information no one else has. You have to listen to me."

So, throwing caution to the wind for the first time in my life, I explain. I tell Agent Denworth about the kidnapped children, about the werewolf compounds, and the many slaves to the werewolf disease. I explain how only Dasc knows where they all are and the only way to set them free is through him.

"Please," I say softly. I can't remember the last time I used the word. "Help us."

Agent Denworth sits quietly stunned for a long moment studying me. Eventually she rises and tells me to wait while she enters the bedroom. I get a fleeting glance of James sitting on the edge of a bed and Celeste leaning over him before the door is shut again. I've just taken one hell of a chance but this is the best opportunity I may ever get. Dasc has entered dangerous territory and the French are already aware of his presence. They could close the net, tighten the noose, and take him into custody. He wouldn't be free to make more werewolves or start another Gathering of small children. Surely if anyone could get him to talk and reveal the locations of the other compounds, it would be the noble class dragons.

Several minutes pass before the door opens once more and Agent Denworth walks James out free of his handcuffs. She undoes mine next while Celeste has a sour look on her face. As soon as my hands are free, James walks over and rests a hand on my shoulder.

"I cut a deal, Genna," he says quietly. "I'm ending this."

As much as I like the thought of it myself, I still don't know if I can trust the IMS here. Once they do have Dasc, what happens to us? What happens to the rest of the werewolves?

"What kind of deal?"

He looks a bit sad as he says, "I can't tell you."

"Why not?"

"Just trust me."

That's not the kind of answer I like. "And if things go sideways?"

"I've taken care of that too."

I give him a sharp look but he just turns to Celeste. "We're ready."

Agent Denworth nods and pulls out a cell phone. "Fill Celeste in on the specifics. I'll call in backup for this little operation of ours."

Despite how agitated Celeste appears about this whole ordeal, she listens with rapt attention as James explains where and when we are to meet Dasc, what precautions he'll take, and what code phrases are to be used. Agent Denworth comes back after making her phone calls lays out the plan for the tactical teams.

Twenty minutes later, James and I have been suited with hidden microphones and leave the IMS safe house to walk to our destination. As we stride down the cobblestone streets, past boutiques and bakeries, I let a small bubble of hope swell in my chest as I finally take in the world around me.

"I told them our story," I say. "I don't trust them, but I told them anyway."

"I did too." We pause at an intersection and he stares hard at me. "This is going to work, Genna. We're going to go home."

I don't say anything in reply. I hope he's right. I dread he's wrong.

Evening has fallen by the time we reach the designated restaurant. It's a quaint place with colorful wallpaper and small round tables stuffed into the main area. There's a thin crowd inside just past the dinner hour. We walk up to the bar and ask for a "drink with bite." The bartender, a man with a curly mustache, nods at us and gestures silently to the door behind him. We take it and descend a flight of stairs to a dimly lit basement.

Then we wait.

The minutes tick by and I find myself inspecting every inch of the basement in the meantime. There's a locked door that blends into the cement walls, a filthy sewer grate, and a stained floor drain. Apart from that, the level is bare. I don't like it. There aren't enough exits for my taste. It feels like a prison cell. Sort of smells like one too despite the restaurant upstairs. I begin to pace and James does the same. A lot is counting on this going right. Our lives for one. The lives of the other werewolves out there for another.

The locked door clicks on the other side of the room.

James and I come to a swift halt and wait motionless as the door creaks open. Two figures slip inside. They take a few steps into the basement but then stop at a distance from us.

"Mercury rises." It's Dasc.

"As talaria takes flight," I answer.

In an instant I can feel Dasc's presence surround me as if telling me everything's okay. Relief and warmth swells in my chest as he walks forward but his companion lingers back in the shadows.

Dasc embraces me like a daughter. "Finally, something went right."

"What's happened?" I ask. "Why did you call us here?"

He takes a step back and takes the measure of both of us. "There's a traitor in our midst."

My stomach flips. He couldn't possibly know. I narrow my eyes. "A traitor?"

He nods and plants his hands on his waist. "One of our

outposts was destroyed, the one that watched over Echidna's old home in Greece. I don't know how it was discovered, except to think that it was betrayed from the inside. Echidna's forces have been moving and I don't know who I can trust in Europe anymore."

I get it now. I'd loose a breath of relief if it wouldn't give me away. "So you wanted someone from outside the continent."

He smiles. "That's my girl. Always sharp as a tack."

"So what now?"

"You help me find out what happened to our outpost and sniff out any traitors amongst our own."

He doesn't know about us. As for any other traitors and an outpost destroyed—I don't know what to make of that except that it turns my stomach. How am I supposed to honor my promise to Alex if the compounds are being destroyed before I can even find them?

But Dasc isn't the only reason I'm here. I look pointedly at his companion lingering behind him. Dasc notices and motions whoever it is forward.

"How rude of me, I haven't introduced our guest," he says. "This is Erebus."

I come face to face with the other half of my reason for coming to this place. The key to finding the Magi and a cure. He's here and not exactly what I'm expecting. He looks more like a slimy businessman than a werewolf hunting Magi. Tall, stick thin, greased-back hair, and a pointed nose, he's not an intimidating figure in the least.

"This is the one I've been telling you about," Dasc says to Erebus. "This is Genna."

Erebus makes a low sweeping bow and murmurs, "Dark Whisper."

Dasc doesn't bother introducing James as if he doesn't even exist.

"Erebus managed to escape Greece but was forced into France of all places," Dasc explains. "We need to get out of here and I'm going to need your help."

"We're at your pleasure," James says—the code phrase.

The world suddenly starts to move very fast and very slow at the same time. A second before the door at the top of the stairs opens, Dasc flicks his eyes towards it and then to James as if realizing something isn't right. Then the door blasts open above and Celeste jumps down. Before she hits the floor, a bright light encases her and she lands not as a woman but as a noble class dragon. Her white scales are near luminescent in the dark basement. She has to duck low of the ceiling and her membrane wings unfurl over her back as far as they will go, scrapping the wood joists overhead. Dazzling, sharp fangs are bared as she hisses in Dasc's direction.

In her wake, a flood of IMS agents come hurtling down the stairs. Dasc makes a sudden move to dash for the hidden door in the wall but finds a jet of flames blocking his way. Celeste snarls and maneuvers about to block any escape he might try to make that way again. I back away from the wave of agents and position myself in front of Dasc. I want them to honor their agreement. I need him alive—for now.

Agent Denworth pushes through to the front of the line of agents with her gun hoisted.

Then I realize it's not a bio-mech gun. None of the agents are carrying the dragon designed gun meant to disable but not kill. No, every single one of them are carrying actual guns for the sole purpose of killing.

We've been double crossed. Something I saw coming miles away.

"There's nowhere to run," Celeste says behind us. "Give yourselves up and no harm will come to you."

That's certainly not what it looks like to me. No, this looks like a trap that we've walked right into. I had let myself think for a second that Agent Denworth might actually be on our side. I guess I was wrong and it's going to cost us everything.

In response to Celeste's command, Agent Denworth takes aim at me.

"What are you doing?" Celeste demands, seeing the same thing I do.

"Oh, we're not taking prisoners today."

"Wait!" Dasc pushes around me and walks directly up to Agent Denworth, ignoring the many guns following his movements. "I'll surrender if you promise not to harm my children."

He gestures over his shoulder to James and me. I can't help but feel my hackles rise at being called his *children*. I don't belong to him. I'll never belong to him.

Agent Denworth lowers her gun and the other agents hold their own a little more loosely.

"You'd do that for them?" she asks as if amazed by this generous turn. "After everything, you'd give yourself up for them?"

"Of course."

I don't know what Dasc is playing at but I don't believe him for a second. He's just trying to play a card to get out of this himself. He knows he's been cornered. This isn't some act out of love. It's an act to buy himself time.

"Well then." Agent Denworth holsters her gun with a sigh. What is she doing? "That's really excellent to know, Lycaon."

She smiles but it's not the smile of an IMS agent—not anymore. The change happens so suddenly there isn't time for anyone to react. One second she's Agent Denworth, the next she has teeth like a shark, slit eyes, and sharp claws on the ends of her fingers.

A lamia.

My heart hammers as all of Dasc's warnings come to fruition in the most inopportune of times. The forward guard to herald Echidna's imminent arrival has appeared. It's started. The war has finally begun. And here, now, when Dasc is the most vulnerable he's ever been. One fell swoop and she could wipe out the most potent weapon against Echidna and my last hope of finding the other werewolves.

One quick thinking agent manages to fire at her but she doesn't even flinch. No, she takes those sharp claws of hers and rips them across Dasc's throat.

"NO!" I scream as blood sprays.

Dasc slumps to the ground.

The next moment chaos erupts as the agents realize there's a monster in their midst and not just any monster— a lamia. Their gunfire shatters the air and flames wreath the ceiling above us as Celeste joins the fray. James and I throw ourselves to the ground to try to avoid the bullets flying in every direction. As the lamia starts ripping through the agents like wheat, I look through the flames and bright spurts of gunfire to find Erebus trying to make a run for the hidden door. He manages to get close enough to grab the handle before he's riddled with bullets by an agent on the fringes of the lamia's rampage. He falls to the floor just like Dasc did. Dead.

My ears ring and everything moves in slow motion as I feel James tug on my arm. We run with hands and arms covering our heads as the wooden joists catch fire, Celeste roars, the agents continue to fire, and the lamia laughs amidst her slaughter. I grab a fallen gun on instinct and run at a crouch away from the devastation. With the stairs blocked, we go the only way we can. Working together we rip off the sewer grate and slip inside. Surrounded by filthy darkness, we run blindly along trying to put as much distance between us and that basement.

My nose fills with rotten, foul things, and my shoes splash through stagnant water. I keep running, the scene of the fight before my eyes, until reality hits me.

Dasc is dead. He was the key to finding the others, but then that other part of me feels a weight lifting off my shoulders.

He's dead. I let out a delirious laugh for a moment that echoes in the storm sewer.

"James!" I whisper. "James, he's . . ."

But I realize his footsteps are faltering in the dark. I stop and wait for him to catch up. My hands grope through the darkness until I manage to grab his arm.

"What's wrong?"

His breath comes in painful sounding rasps. "Let's get . . . outside."

My heart thunders in my ears and I keep a grip on his arm, wandering blindly until pale light draws us towards an exit. A heavy grate blocks the end of the tunnel but after a few tries I manage to shove it open. We emerge beneath a bridge, a river coursing through the city before our feet. The second we're free of the tunnel, James collapses onto the cement that channels the water. I drop to my knees next to him feeling suddenly feverish.

"I guess I drew the short stick," he wheezes.

He pulls back the collar of his shirt to reveal a bleeding graze from one of the bullets. It doesn't look deep but there's a nasty smell to it that I recognize.

A shock goes through me. "The bullets were coated in wolfsbane."

James nods and rests against the cement culvert. I stagger away from him.

There is no cure for wolfsbane. I've seen the horrid effects of it before when it killed so many of my friends in the compound, when it took Alex. Once in the blood, there's nothing anyone can do.

James will die.

"Guess I'm not going home after all," he says.

"Don't say that." I shake my head. "Don't you say that."

"It's okay. I knew you'd make it. You were always the strong one."

"How did this happen?" I shout and grasp at my hair. Unbidden tears escape my eyes and everything that's been festering inside me for years comes crawling out. "*Why?*"

I'm so distraught that I hardly register the sound of footsteps coming up through the tunnel. Choking back a sob, I heft the gun and point it down the tunnel ready for whoever is stupid enough to have followed us. There's an odd gurgling sound along with the splash of footsteps.

"Why indeed?" a faint voice says as the figure emerges.

One hand clutching his bleeding throat, Dasc steps out of the storm sewer with his eyes fixed on me. The world falls silent as I take him in, still alive after having his throat slashed open by the lamia.

"Don't look so surprised," Dasc says, his words slightly gurgled as he talks around the blood in his throat. "People have been trying to kill me for years. I don't die easily."

Then he lifts a gun of his own and aims it at me. "So, who do I have to thank for that bit of betrayal?"

I blink and don't move.

A weak voice on the ground beside us says, "It was me."

I close my eyes against the building pain racing through me as I begin to understand.

"I made a deal," James continues and struggles to his feet to face Dasc directly. The barrel of Dasc's gun swings to him. "Genna didn't know the deal I made with the IMS. I hid it from her. I've wanted you dead for a long, long time. I became very good at hiding it, you know. You never suspected anything."

"I always thought you smelled a bit rank," Dasc says dully and his eyes shift to me as if he knows all too well that James hasn't been working alone.

James must sense it too, because he goes on. "I made sure Genna brought me here where you'd be away from your followers. I knew this would be the best place to take you down. She's been your loyal Dark Whisper all this time. Do you have any idea how hard this has been? To live alongside her when she does everything you ask?"

Dasc's eyes bore into mine and I can feel his presence smothering me.

"Is this true?" he asks.

The force behind his question hits me in the gut like a punch and I can feel the truth wanting to slip free of my lips.

Tell the truth. Tell the truth.

My mouth opens and I made an odd sort of sound as I fight the compulsion he feeds into me. I look to James and can see the glint of hope there. He had planned this. This was his contingency all along if things went sideways. One of us has to make it home, even if that means sacrificing the other. But then he must have known this would happen as well, that Dasc would compel the truth from us.

And yet . . . everything James said was true in a manner. I didn't know the specifics of the deal he made with the IMS. He did insist on coming with me to France. And I *have* been Dasc's loyal Whisper as I played to be. It's been difficult for both of us for me to be the person I needed to be to survive.

"It's true," I whisper. "All of it."

Dasc adjusts the hand on his throat and gestures with his gun to the one I'm holding. His piercing eyes rake me as he says, "If there is rot, we cut it out. The pack survives."

I realize what he's asking and now I know why Zeredah wanted to test me, to see if I could fool him. Because in this moment, it takes everything within me to raise the gun in my hand and point it at James without flinching, without showing a trace of mercy, or hesitation. James faces it in the same manner without blinking any eye. His skin is pale and sweat gathers on his forehead as the wolfsbane takes its toll.

But he stands resolute. He will not beg or plead. What is offered to him now is a merciful relief from the pain he's enduring and will endure until it drains the life out of him. This is also his sacrifice. Trying to kill Dasc in this moment—something I don't even know how to achieve—would make such a sacrifice pointless. He'd just kill me too. I have to endure. I have to continue on. I have to make it home.

"I trusted you," I breathe, unable to raise my voice any higher. "You were my friend. And you betrayed me."

Because we were both supposed to make it home in the end.

I wipe the back of my hand across my nose. James closes his eyes.

And I fire.

Day . . .

I've been a ghost for a long time. Some days I wonder if my soul has left my body—if I still have a soul after what I've done. I left any shred of humanity I had back in Paris beside that river.

Each day moves like fog rolling through a bleak and barren landscape. Nothing really sticks anymore. I walk and talk like a normal human being but it's like I'm watching a movie and not participating myself.

The only thing left is the promise I made to James—that one of us make it home.

After we escaped Paris, Dasc and I went into hiding as he healed. It's been weeks of eavesdropping and gathering information as we huddle in Switzerland avoiding IMS agents and Echidna's monsters alike. So far nothing has come out of France about Dasc, the battle in the basement, the lamia, any of it. I've no doubt they're covering it up since they blew it. They had Dasc literally in their hands and he slipped away. Their efforts to save face also mean that they wouldn't have told my father about my appearance either. That thought weighs heavily on my mind.

After my performance murdering my only true friend, Dasc has shared more with me. If I had been his favorite, I've become even more so after helping him escape. I've learned about some other compounds but never enough, never all of it. Each time I look at Dasc's face, I want to cut him up into tiny pieces. But he doesn't die easily and he's been more alert and wary than ever since that horrible day in France when all the color bled out of the world.

We eventually slip out of Switzerland and head north. During our stealthy journey, Dasc is quiet and deep in thought. He doesn't mention anything about seeking out the Magi again. I don't know if that hope died with Erebus or if it's something he's not willing to talk about with me. All he really says anymore is that the war has begun. The lamia have reappeared. Echidna is on the move.

"We need more," I hear him muttering to himself sometimes. Meanwhile I'm thinking about putting an icepick through his skull.

We reach London near the summer solstice and Rosalyn meets us at an old inn along the Thames. I don't know why Dasc has summoned her now but she preens when we meet her, clearly seeing this as a bump in her importance. We gather in our room—Dasc has been sleeping in the bed while I take the floor as his ever present guard—and Dasc sits heavily on the edge of the mattress.

"My dear girls," he begins. "The war has come upon us

at last but we must be ready. Our forces have been severely weakened and there is not much hope in overcoming the darkness that will surely fall once Echidna makes her appearance. There is a task you must do for me while I bolster our numbers."

I don't like the sound of that. It sounds like the Gathering is about to begin anew.

"Of course," Rosalyn says, clinging to his every word.

"My bite may have weakened Echidna but she's still alive. Our greatest weapon is not enough to stop her, and we can't afford to face her only to fail. I need you to find a creature for me that may be the key to putting an end to Echidna for good. You must find the bean nighe."

"The washer woman," I murmur. An old Scotland creature that's so rare it's almost a myth to people like us. A creature that knows when, where, and how people will die.

"She's the only one who can tell us how to kill Echidna."

And . . . how to kill Dasc himself. That's when I understand why Rosalyn is here. If there's still any doubt about my loyalties, Dasc wants someone he knows is loyal to the very end to be here—to stop me if I could have my way.

"I would entrust this task to no one else," he continues. "But I would warn you, this task may be an impossible feat. There have been rumors of a bean nighe spotted in Scotland once more but there's no way to know where she will be or how to find her. I'm counting on both of you. Do not fail me."

Rosalyn looks like she'd be willing to throw herself on a sword if he asked her. Of course she'll be putting her all into this.

"And what about you?" I ask. "Where are you heading now?"

He begins to pace. "I've been thinking that it's time for a new plan of action. We need numbers but we don't have the time for proper training like you girls received."

I imagine another girl grinding her teeth or throttling Dasc so I don't do it myself.

"I think it's time I returned to the States and . . . widened the fold, so to speak. I fancy I'll return to Minnesota. There are excellent candidates in the area well suited for the task ahead. And I do miss the coffee at Java Jitters in Moose Lake."

My gut plummets as I realize what he's doing. Even with Rosalyn here, it's another precaution to make sure that I do what I'm supposed to. The threat is clear to me. Find this bean nighe for him, or he'll pay my father a visit. Maybe visit Rosalyn's brother as well. He'll be there and he'll be waiting like a snake in the grass.

"We'll find the bean nighe," I say. "We'll find out how to kill Echidna."

His smile is that of a wolf. "That's my girl."

The lingering threat of what might happen to our families remains as Dasc eventually parts ways to head back to the States. It remains with me as Rosalyn and I make our way north. It's at the forefront of my thoughts as we reach Edinburgh and check ancient libraries for a hint of how to find one of the most elusive beings on the planet. A month ticks by as we hunt for clues and use the resources at the Scotland werewolf compound without any success.

Zeredah manages to sneak me messages via other shapeshifters to let me know how my own compound in

Canada is doing as well as reports of Dasc's movements. By July I hear he's back in Moose Lake but has made no move on my father. A month ticks by, then another, and I hear he's begun turning the populace. My father's fate hangs in the forefront of my mind every day as Rosalyn and I continue our desperate hunt for the bean nighe. Not only do I need to fulfill this mission to find a way to kill Dasc, but to ensure he doesn't kill my father out of my failure.

It isn't until the end of October that we get our first stroke of luck. While out hunting for leads in one of the local pubs, I overhear a man raving about a crazy old bat telling him his best friend was going to die. The onlookers laugh and shake their heads. The man has several empty mugs and bottles before him. His story is being taken for nonsensical drunken raving but I know better.

"I'm telling ye!" the man thunders when someone flat out tells him he's a radge. "She said 'e'd die drowning on cliffs o' despair! And 'e's dead, 'e is! Died just—just last night!" He begins to howl in his misery. "Drowned in 'is own bathtub!"

The barkeep eventually comes over to cut him off and help him to a taxi outside. I slip after them and before the taxi can drive away, I grab the open door and lean in to the man still blubbering uncontrollably.

"I believe you," I say quickly. The driver gives me a foul look for holding them up. "Where did you talk to this woman?"

"Wha'?" He turns his bleary, watery eyes to me dumbfounded.

"The woman who said your friend was going to die. Where did you talk to her?"

He points vaguely into the distance as if that makes it perfectly clear. "The ruins south of Edinburgh. The big . . . the big ones." He makes a rainbow motion with his hands to describe just how big. "The abbey."

I've become familiar enough with Scotland to know what he's talking about. "Holyrood Abbey? Is that what you're talking about?"

He makes a click and winks, giving me the double point. "That's the one."

"When was this?"

"'Bout a week ago?"

The driver honks the horn. I slam the door and take a step back so it can pull away. That's about all I was going to get out of that man anyway. But it's enough. It's a place to start at the very least.

"Things are looking up, I take it?" a Mediterranean accent says behind me, rather out of place for my current surroundings.

I turn around to find Zeredah leaning against the wall of the pub. She's in her home form with silky black hair, dark beige skin, and the usual smirk as if she finds everything around her humorous.

"I didn't expect to see you here," I say. "Why aren't you back at the compound?"

She pushes off from the side of the pub and walks casually over. She's a lot taller than me in her home form. "The place is well in hand without me there, and I wanted to share a bit of news with you personally."

Zeredah lets that settle for a moment as if trying to build the anticipation. I don't ask her what news she's brought with her to Scotland. She'll tell me without prompting.

She sidles a little closer and whispers, "Dasc was captured by the IMS."

I blink. There's a hollow ringing in my ears.

"*What?*" I ask breathlessly.

"He was discovered while in Moose Lake. Sounds like it was quite the show, actually." She smiles as if enjoying dragging this out. "Your father was there—don't worry, he's fine. I heard Dasc tried to have him killed by one of my fellow idiots that went dark side. It didn't take though."

"He's okay," I whisper as if saying the words any louder will break them.

"He's fine thanks to a couple of redheads. The girl . . . what was her name . . ."

An old, old memory of playing with two squirrelly twins surfaces.

"Phoenix," I say.

"Yes, that was it. How'd you know?"

"What did she do?"

"Emptied a clip of wolfsbane bullets into Dasc." Zeredah chuckles and rocks on her heels. "While surrounded by a group of zombified werewolves Dasc had turned no less. Tough girl. She's got balls."

"But he survived," I say darkly. Of course he did.

"Hospitalized and taken into custody. The IMS has him now." Zeredah rests a hand on my shoulder. "You're free, Genna. You can go home."

Home.

The word swells like a balloon in my chest. I haven't felt this light in—well, since I was seven years old and riding a bicycle with a wooden sword. My father's alive and he never gave up on me.

No more running. No more lies. No more watching my friends die.

But then I start to think quickly, pushing aside happier thoughts as I sift through the data in my head as usual. There's a standing order for all Whispers that in the event Dasc is captured, we are to free him. I sure as hell won't but I'm not the only Whisper out there. How long until one of the others figures out he's been captured? How long until they manage his escape? An entire clip of wolfsbane bullets didn't end him. If he's freed once more, there will be no stopping him. And nothing will keep my father safe then.

"Who else knows?" I ask quietly.

Zeredah gives me an odd look. "I thought you'd be thrilled about this."

"Who else knows?" I repeat.

"I'm not sure. I figure the watch guard will find out eventually. Apart from that, there's no telling who else found out."

"Do what you can to keep the knowledge of his capture under wraps."

She gives an odd jerk being taken aback. "You aren't going home, are you?"

The decision weighs heavily on me to the point I feel like I've sunken a foot into the ground. I could run home right now. I could leave this wretched life behind and return to my father. But if I did that and the worst happened, if Dasc was freed, I would be powerless to stop him and James's sacrifice would have been for nothing. I close my eyes as the vivid image of ending my friend's life haunts me for the millionth time. It'll never stop haunting me.

One of us has to make it home.

But not yet.

"I can't. Not until I see this through."

Zeredah breathes a sigh and crosses her arms. "You're one tough bastard, Genna."

Ignoring her idea of a compliment, I say, "Keep an eye on him, will you?"

"I'll do you one better." Her smirk returns and a glimmer enters her eyes. "I'm not just here to give you good news. I'm on my way to suggest to a bunch of selkies that they relocate to Minnesota to offer protection to a certain local resident."

It's my turn to be taken aback. "Selkies? How are you going to manage that?"

She winks. "We all have our secrets, Dark Whisper. And I owe it to a friend to see this through."

"You aren't ever going to give me a straight answer, are you?"

"Never."

She sticks her hands in her jacket pockets and makes to walk away into the growing darkness.

"Wait," I call after her. "I've been meaning to ask, what ever happened to your contact in France? It seemed awfully convenient that the IMS happened to be waiting in the area where we were to meet. I can't help but wonder why they were there."

Zeredah stops and looks over her shoulder. "I hope you aren't suggesting I led you into a trap, love."

"Did you?"

"Genna, if I ever decided to lure you into a trap, you wouldn't even know it. Tah!" She waves and strides off to be swallowed by the night.

Not satisfied with her answer in the least, I return to the pub and find Rosalyn attempting to pick up news on the opposite side near the bar. I motion for her to follow and we leave the pub together to walk down the rutted lane outside.

"What'd you find out?" Rosalyn asks.

I smile into the crisp evening air thinking of my father, of Dasc in chains, and freedom waiting whenever I choose to seek it. I say none of it to Rosalyn. It's my secret to cherish for the time being. But it's time to finish what I started—for Alex, for Susan, for James.

"Let's go find us a bean nighe."

THE ADVENTURE CONTINUES . . .

Get news about the next book in the series at:
brightway-books.com

Find exclusive content at:
bethanyhelwig.com

ABOUT THE AUTHOR

Bethany Helwig lives in a small town in Minnesota. When not working as a paralegal, she writes fantasy novels, composes music, tries her hand at art, and enjoys the madness that comes with participating in various fandoms.